BRIDE FOR SALE

There was only one thing that Squire Quentin Marshall loved more than his enchanting daughter Annemarie. That one thing was money.

Now the money that he wanted so badly and needed even more could be his if Annemarie wed the licentious but filthy-rich Lord Blakewell.

On the other hand, Lord Blakewell's very distant and disquietingly unconventional cousin Seth had arrived from America with a business proposition too tempting to turn down.

These two men were bidding everything they had for Annemarie's hand—but only one had the key to her heart. . . .

ROMANTIC ENCOUNTERS

Heir to
Vengeance

Roberta Eckert

A SIGNET BOOK

NEW AMERICAN LIBRARY
A DIVISION OF PENGUIN BOOKS USA INC.

NAL BOOKS ARE AVAILABLE AT QUANTITY DISCOUNTS WHEN USED TO
PROMOTE PRODUCTS OR SERVICES. FOR INFORMATION PLEASE WRITE TO
PREMIUM MARKETING DIVISION, NEW AMERICAN LIBRARY, 1633 BROADWAY,
NEW YORK, NEW YORK 10019.

SIGNET TRADEMARK REG. U.S. PAT. OFF. AND FOREIGN COUNTRIES
REGISTERED TRADEMARK—MARCA REGISTRADA
HECHO EN DRESDEN, TN., U.S.A.

SIGNET, SIGNET CLASSIC, MENTOR, ONYX, PLUME, MERIDIAN
and NAL BOOKS are published by New American Library, a division
of Penguin Books USA Inc., 1633 Broadway, New York, NY 10019

First Printing, March, 1990

1 2 3 4 5 6 7 8 9

PRINTED IN THE UNITED STATES OF AMERICA

To Earl
and life's journey taken

Author's Note

The incident of Americans marrying into the English aristocracy is not unusual.

The son of the Duke and Duchess of Marlborough married Jenny Jerome, an American. Jenny's grandmother was a full-blooded Iroquois. The child of that union became England's greatest prime minister.

That he was half-American and part-American Indian was always a source of amusement and pride to Sir Winston Churchill.

1

The unpleasant atmosphere of the overflowing taproom was becoming more oppressive by the moment. The lack of air was stifling. The dying September storm sent gusts of wind that rattled the diamond-paned windows and sent puffs of smoke out from the faulty fireplace. The smell of stale ale and too many unwashed bodies only added to the discomfort of the stranded wayfarers.

Voices rose and fell in endless demands from the complaining patrons who vied for service from too few barmaids. The delighted innkeeper may have been harried but he smiled at the brisk business that resulted from the travelers' inconvenience. The sound of his voice carried over the general din as he excitedly issued orders to servants and postilions alike. Confusion reigned throughout the inn while he attempted to accommodate the exceptional number of travelers seeking to spend the night.

The innkeeper's red-faced, portly wife bustled about desperately trying to fill orders for food. Supplies were being fast depleted. Ham served earlier in thick slices was now offered in small, thin portions. Roasts were now cut into tiny bits, smothered with gravy, and poured over bread. Fortunately, there seemed to be no shortage of ale or wine, and its consumption added to the increasing clamor of the patrons' demanding voices.

In the dimmest corner of the room a lone gentleman rested against the straight settle and observed the scene with keen interest. Being more fortunate to have arrived earlier, he had partaken of an adequate meal in the company of his traveling companion and he relaxed with the knowledge that a private bedchamber was secured.

He was glad just to sit and watch, for this very afternoon he had landed his ship, *Columbia,* out of Savannah, and was weary from the long voyage and the heavy seas that had kept them off shore for three days.

The fierce storm had prevented outbound ships from leaving Southampton harbor and inbound ships from docking. When the vessels had finally made anchor, the roads were found to be a sea of quagmire and therefore impassable.

The American gentleman smiled slightly, as it occurred to him that the hard straight-back settle on which he sat would provide an uncomfortable bed for some poor guest who would consider himself fortunate to have it.

He sat in silence, speaking only to order another mulled wine. His low, resonant voice carried a distinct American accent, causing several guests to cast him inquisitive looks. If the gentleman marked such curious glances, he gave no indication, and soon those who noted him turned once more to their own endeavors.

Since the clientele in the crowded taproom comprised only men, the buxom barmaid obviously singled out this dark-haired traveler on whom to lavish her attention. Her decided and appreciative feminine gaze critically appraised his appearance. He was tall and well-built, to be sure, but it was his face that gave him a mysterious aura. It was a uniquely handsome face with high, chiseled cheekbones, a classic nose, and pale, smoky eyes, which were the exceptional gray-green color often found among Creek Indians. His eyes were both soft and intense, and had been duly inherited from his

Creek grandmother. The barmaid, of course, had no knowledge of his heritage, but it was obvious to her that he was a gentleman, and a compelling one.

He had a rugged quality, an underlying intensity that belied his seemingly relaxed manner. It was as if he were a sleek panther resting patiently, yet every muscle poised to spring into action.

The barmaid brushed against him as she sat a mulled wine before him. "I'm Nora, sir. Can I get ye *anything* else ye might be wanting?" She leaned over his table, displaying more than a little of her ample white breasts.

His eyes flickered a moment and he offered a slow smile. "Not tonight. It is sleep that beckons me," he said softly in his distinct American twang.

Nora removed his plate with a flourish. " 'Tis a wonder you were men enough to win the war," she chided.

A soft, melodious laugh escaped his lips as he tossed a crown upon the table. "We saved our strength to fight another day," he said lightly.

Nora tossed her bright-red curls disdainfully and flounced away. A pout appeared on her lips as she thought to seek another gallant to pay for her charms this evening, but none half so handsome or intriguing, she was certain. A bit high and mighty to decline her offer, she thought, Although he might be dressed like a gentleman, she scoffed, with a fine ruby signet ring on his finger, his hands were those that had known work.

Staring a moment at the barmaid's swaying hips, Seth Blakewell shrugged, then rose from the uncomfortable bench and made his way easily through the thronging crowd. He exuded such a powerful physical presence that the other patrons unconsciously stepped aside for him. It was not just his strapping physique but an aura of respect he seemed to command.

He threw on a beautifully handmade leather weather cape, smiling to himself as he remembered the careworn hands that had so lovingly fashioned it. Sure that the likes of it had never been seen in England, he proudly drew it closer to his body as he stepped out into the night air.

The ground was still a sea of mud squishing beneath his boots with each step he took. The rain had finally stopped and the sky appeared to be clearing, for he noticed a few tiny stars flickering occasionally among the fleeting clouds. The wind was still high, but the crisp, cool air felt good as he took a deep breath. Most of his life had been spent out in the open, and the brisk air stirred him with pleasure as he crossed the yard to the stables.

The lanterns cast a warm glow in the stable as Seth stepped inside. Angus stood at the flanks of a large gray mare checking the merits of the animal. The tall, rugged man with unruly red hair looked up, his blue eyes dancing with ready humor.

" 'Evening Seth," Angus Grey said as he straightened up.

"Good evening, Angus," Seth replied. "Find any suitable?"

"Hell, no! They're nothing but a bunch of nags," Angus said, shaking his head. "None will do. The decent horses belong to the other guests. We can get to London, but then we'll have to acquire suitable mounts there. These English sure ride sorry-looking animals. Don't speak much for their horse sense."

Seth smiled and nodded to his friend. "Go, get rest. I'm weary as you must be. We'll find some horses to get us to London. Just think, two country boys riding up to London town. Maybe it will turn us into proper city gents."

Angus nodded in amused agreement. "I'll await your summons on the *Columbia*. Remember you ain't going to turn me into a fancy, dandified gentleman." He laughed as he turned to walk out into the night.

"Might do you a good turn to learn to dress like a proper gentleman. You're likely to run for governor someday," Seth called out after him. He heard Angus laugh.

Seth continued to smile as he watched his companion disappear into the black night, grateful that Angus had insisted on accompanying him. Recollecting the long night when they had discussed the merits of this venture, Seth walked slowly back to the inn. Doubts began to crowd his mind.

Revenge, he had hotly debated with Angus, was not his aim. He wished to see his true inheritance. Alone with his thoughts, and his conscience, he had to acknowledge that now vengeance played a growing role in his considerations. Each experience he'd seen since leaving the *Columbia* confirmed his notion that revenge was not only just, but necessary. He recalled the crested coach that had nearly run him over after he disembarked from his ship. There was also the arrogant attitude of the few minor gentry demanding immediate attention at the inn. This rankled his ideals concerning privilege and touched on the injustice that had brought him to England.

Entering the inn, he slowly edged his way through the noisy patrons and made his way up the narrow, rickety stairs to the cramped room that would be his until he left for London. The obscure inn had been chosen to provide a certain anonymity. This reasoning made him smile. Still, he was lucky to have secured any space, as he attracted attention every time he opened his mouth. Although women found his accent intriguing, he had more need of invisibility than companionship at this particular moment. He wanted to choose the time and place to announce his existence.

Perhaps Angus is right in wishing to remain aboard the *Columbia*, he mused. Angus had said Seth could be the brave who scouted ahead of a war party. "I'll allow you the privilege of being the 'wolf warrior,' while I sleep in a bed I know has no fleas,'' Angus had teased.

Ducking his head to avoid the low lintel, Seth entered the small whitewashed room and threw off his fine leather cape. The fire in the grate sent out a cheery welcome and he was glad for that, for the gray, wet, and chilly weather seemed to have seeped into his bones. Carefully he bolted the door, removed a leather-wrapped packet from inside his coat, and placed it upon the bed. He withdrew a silver inlaid pistol from his belt and set it on top of the packet. Walking slowly to the window, he leaned against the frame and looked out into the black night. The lights from the inn shone into the empty yard below. There was nothing else visible, so he closed the drape with a quick stroke.

He stripped off his boots and outer clothes and poured water into the basin. His tall, tanned, hard-muscled body glistened as he washed with the lukewarm water. It was a body of prime manly perfection. The broad shoulders, strong, dark-haired chest, which tapered to a flat stomach, his narrow waist, and his well-muscled limbs were evidence of his many years of active hard work. His movements were easy and had a casual, fluid motion that separated him from his English cousins and indicated, as clearly as his speech, that he was an American.

Shivering slightly in the cool damp air, he slipped into a flannel nightshirt and climbed into the bed, which smelled of musty straw. He remembered the nights he had slept among the sweet-smelling Georgia pine. Stretching out under the covers, he was grateful for the warming pan placed in the bed, but his thoughts quickly returned to his native, warmer Georgia. A worried frown crossed his face as he wondered if his mother was well. It seemed so long ago, yet it was last July when he had received her urgent summons to return to Savannah. He had been working at Riverview, his plantation on the Altamaha River, when the message came. He had ridden all night to reach Savannah.

Yellow fever! God, that terrifying illness that struck so suddenly and without mercy to any age or gender. His father had been taken with it, and died in three days. Seth softly sighed and closed his eyes against the lingering pain, for he had loved his father and keenly felt the loss.

The image of his mother appeared in his mind. He admired her as much as he had his quiet, industrious father. She was tall, with a grace and dignity born of overcoming the obstacles of prejudice. Alma Sorenson was half Creek Indian and half Swedish, had married John Blakewell in 1779 just short of a year after his arrival from England. They had struggled together as equal partners to develop the flourishing plantation. Alma's quiet courage and kindness had eventually won her the acceptance she deserved, but she always carried a certain reserve that was so easily understood by her son.

Alma had brought the leather packet to him shortly after his father's funeral. He recalled her soft voice as she explained the events that had led to his father's arrival in America. The great care with which she unwrapped the soft packet and removed the contents indicated the value she placed upon them. The items included a purse of gold crowns, legal papers, and a ruby ring. Taking the proffered papers, Seth carefully read. Slowly, he raised his eyes to his mother's with the realization they contained the information that John Blakewell was the heir to the Earl of Chathram. He fingered the signet ring and asked, ''The gold?''

''Blood money,'' she replied.

John Blakewell had spoken little of his English home, and now Seth, almost at the doorstep of his father's aristocratic English family, was beginning to understand the reason.

Stretched out on the narrow bed of the Sea Belle Inn, Seth

turned the ring on his finger and questioned his commitment to meet his father's family. He was naturally curious, but the real reason he would, of course, was that his mother had implored him to do so. "You must go, Seth, for me at least," she said.

"I want you to see if his father lives, and if not, find his younger brother. I want them to learn he survived his betrayal, fared well, and had a fine son who is the rightful heir. I do not like the lie that stains his name. He was a fine man, but he never cared to return to clear his name or claim his inheritance. Your father abhorred the outcome of revealing the crime. My Creek heritage does not allow me to rest while his honor remains defamed. I ask you to go and exonerate him. Whether you should claim your rightful heritage, I cannot say. That is for you to decide."

Following the emotional exchange with his mother, Seth visited Angus Grey, relating the same tale his mother had told him, the tale of betrayal and plotted murder. Angus seethed with outrage.

"You mean his own brother allowed him to take the blame for the shooting over some card game?" Angus asked incredulously.

"Yes, aided and abetted by the son of a country squire by the name of Marshall, and on my father's way to Southampton they had him waylaid and impressed into the navy. Savannah, as you know, was still held by the English. Before the ship docked in Savannah, the captain called Father to his cabin. My father was stunned to learn the captain had been given a purse of gold in payment to see that he did not live out the journey. The captain declared he'd never be a party to such a plan, but had falsely agreed, knowing it was best to transport him out of England, for surely someone else would do the deed. The captain gave the purse of gold coins to my father, wished him godspeed, and allowed him to jump ship.''

Angus remained silent, shaking his head in disbelief. ''Will you go, as your mother requests?'' Angus finally asked.

''I must. I have no choice. I will confront his brother. I may even claim my right to the title to avenge my father's betrayal.'' Seth's eyes glittered coldly.

''Your father never desired to go. Why do you? Leave it, Seth. You're not that kind of man. Look at what you've accomplished here. I know, I'm your lawyer. You're a rich man. You don't need it. But if you go, I'll join you. It would be worth it, just to see you all fancied up.'' Angus laughed at the ridiculous idea, trying to lighten the morbid mood of his friend.

Seth smiled lightly and knowingly in return. The image was just as improbable to him as Angus, and he understood his friend well.

''I wonder how the proper earl's family would like to learn the earldom rightfully belongs to an Indian,'' Seth said with a derisive smile. ''Besides, it has nothing to do with seeking any wealth, and you know that!''

''You are a rough-cut American, and that'll be bad enough. I'll go with you. You might just need a strong arm at your side, against that cutthroat family of yours,'' Angus said.

The sound of raucous laughter from the taproom brought Seth's thoughts back to the present with a sudden start. He shifted on the narrow bed, realizing that what had initially begun as a quest to vindicate his father's betrayal was now becoming something else. I must guard myself, he thought, vengeance can lead a man to be careless. Where my father had no reason to suspect he would be betrayed, I know better, and I'll not be caught in any trap, least of all one of my own.

Seth reached over to snuff the flickering candle. The ruby

of the signet ring caught the light and flashed fire.

The following morning dawned sunny and bright and the sky was the intense cobalt blue that October brings before the arrival of November's pale-gray skies. Seth had slept well and felt invigorated by the clear, crisp air. He set briskly about the tasks he had to accomplish. First he wrote to his father's solicitor in London, requesting a meeting, having found the name among his father's papers and wondered if the man was still alive. Then he went in search of horses for the journey and found none suitable. Angus joined in the search, which ended in the hiring of two work horses from a local farmer.

Luckily the fine weather held, so when Angus and Seth started out for London, high spirits prevailed. They both dressed comfortably for the journey in fringed buckskins. As they readied their horses, their appearance caused curious glances, considerable disdain, and even merriment.

English gentlemen, who wore coats so snug they had to have assistance in putting them on, trousers so tight they could barely sit, and collar points so high they couldn't turn their heads, were aghast at such outlandish wearing apparel. Even the young stable boys doubled over in fits of laughter.

"Seems we're causing a stir." Angus chuckled as he secured his saddlebags on the horse. "Let 'em laugh; at least we'll be comfortable and dry," he added as he raised his arm to show the fringe, which was designed to carry off rainwater with his movement.

Nodding, Seth swung up into the saddle. "We'll cause much more of a stir by the time we reach London."

"They can laugh at my buckskins, but damn it, I'm ashamed of the horses we've hired. Pinches my pride a bit," Angus said as he seated himself in his saddle. He sent Seth a look of mock forlorn.

"You do me honor with your sacrifice, Angus. It is my solemn pledge, we'll purchase better when we are settled," Seth said, heading his horse out of the stableyard.

"Settled, what in the blazes does that mean?" Angus teased.

"That, my good friend, only time will tell," Seth replied as they lengthened the stride of their horses and set off for London.

2

Miss Annemarie Marshall smartly maneuvered a fine Irish hunter through intricate paces on the sweeping south meadow. Standing seventeen hands high, the horse was a magnificent, sleek black stallion with a deep chest and perfect slant of shoulder. He answered his rider's every subtle command, holding his head with elegant pride while his powerful haunches allowed the clearing of each fence with ease.

The young lady executed each jump with precision, as though she were an extension of the animal. She impressively sat upon the large animal with the grace and command of an assured horsewoman. The fluid economy of her movements made it obvious she had the strength and ability to command such a splendid horse.

Rounding the last stretch of the course, Annemarie tossed her head, and a melodious sound of laughter escaped her wide smile, bringing a snappy sparkle to her almond-shaped eyes.

"He's a beauty, Mr. McGuire. Well-named, to be sure," she proclaimed with unabashed pride as she reined in the huge mount before the fence on which Patrick McGuire leaned. The head groom was a small wiry man with a weather-lined face and keen eyes that reflected the young woman's enthusiasm.

"Aye, that she is," McGuire cheered, doffing his hat in

approval at the perfectly executed run. "You ride among the best. I've not seen better, and Taliesin knows it. He's your slave . . . do anything you wish. Loyalty makes this breed so outstanding, for he'll answer to only one master. You've earned his devotion. He belongs to you; the match is made."

Resting in the saddle, the young woman smiled with pride and contentment as she reached over to stroke the black mane. "He's wonderful. Thank you, McGuire, for finding him for me. Without your knowledge and guidance I'm not sure I could have won Taliesin."

The trainer knew she spoke the truth, and pride showed in his Celtic eyes while he acknowledged her own ability, which allowed the stallion to accept her. Their eyes met in respected understanding as he nodded, pleased with her compliment.

"I must return it to the stable before Mother arises and I again upset her," she said with a sly smile and shrug of her shoulders.

Patrick McGuire watched the handsome young woman turn the horse and canter away. He admired her ability, spirit, and unconventionality.

After returning Taliesin to the stable and placing the stallion in the care of a groom, Anne strode quickly along the stone walk toward the lovely ivy-covered country manor. With a confident, athletic grace to her step, she slipped in the back entrance, hoping to avoid her mother's inevitable disapproval of the breeches she wore. Being an early-enough hour, she did so with confidence, since her mother rarely rose before ten. Correct in her estimate and timing, she went up to her room unnoticed by most of the servants.

Flora awaited her mistress with a bright smile and curtsy.

"Good morning, Flora. And that it is, for the day is beautiful and my ride was more rewarding than I could have

ever expected. He's the finest and most remarkable horse
I've ever owned," Anne said. Her voice was filled with
excitement, yet held a soft modulated quality that demanded
instant attention.

"I'm glad you find him to your liking. I've seen the beast
and he frightened me to the death. You'd not find me on
his back for love nor gold," the diminutive maid said,
emphatically shaking her head over the frightening aspect
of being seated on such an animal.

"I should hope not! You're so tiny. A lady's small chestnut
would suit you well. Since, to my mother's chagrin, I'm no
dainty miss, my size allows me the pleasure of riding such
a magnificent animal," Anne teased as she began to remove
the masculine clothes she wore.

Flora helped, but a hint of disapproval showed in her eyes.
She was exceedingly fond of her stately mistress and disliked
her totally unacceptable riding clothes. In that sentiment Flora
was in complete agreement with the harping Mrs. Marshall.

Later assisting Miss Anne into a simple cream muslin
gown, Flora admired her mistress's tall and very feminine
figure as she buttoned the numerous tiny pearl buttons. After
brushing her tawny-gold hair until it glowed the color of
sherry, Flora deftly twisted it into a sleek top knot. She
smiled with proprietary approval, for Miss Anne possessed
very beautiful hair and Flora took as much pleasure in
dressing it as if it were her own. She longed to create a less-
severe style, but her no-nonsense mistress would have none
of the affected artifice deemed necessary by most young
ladies.

Flora stepped back as Anne gave a cursory glance at her
tidy reflection and nodded approval. Adjusting her shawl,
Anne proceeded to join her father in the breakfast room.

Quentin Marshall sat at the head of the oval table carefully reading a London paper. Although an adequate country

squire, his interests lay firmly in the world of commerce and politics, and he zealously kept abreast of them both. It was commerce—or precisely the lure of money to be made in some venture—that was his primary interest. Astute enough to know successful ventures often hinged on current politics, he actively pursued both. Not that this devoted study ever culminated in the fervent desire to reap great financial rewards, for he had always been too greedy. Any wise investor knows that calculated restraints must temper chances taken, but Quentin Marshall never let ethics or restraint mar the next vision of great wealth.

Squire Marshall was still a handsome man at fifty-three, with thick graying hair and a large powerful body only slightly turning to thickening fat. His manner was generally pleasant and he could count many people, if not actual friends, as cordial acquaintances. Quentin knew far too well the advantages of connections and presented a favorable impression to those he considered important. There were secrets in his eyes, however, that glittered and hinted at a hidden facet of his nature. Few knew him well.

His business dealings rarely involved his family, although he shared the raising of fine horses with his daughter. This venture was mutually enjoyed.

Squire Marshall greeted his daughter with affection. "Good morning, my dear." He set aside his paper.

Glowing with animation, she returned the greeting. "Good morning, Father. I've just returned from riding the new hunter. He's wonderful! Beyond any I have ever had the pleasure of owning. Thank you for purchasing him." Anne dropped a kiss on his forehead as she moved to the sideboard.

"Humph, 'tis happy I am you like Taliesin. Thought he might be too much animal for you, but McGuire assures me not. He tells me you have a perfect match. We will have some splendid times with him in hunt," he sighed. "But you spend too much time with the horses, according to your mother. You must abide her wishes and act more like the young lady you are,'' he added. These words were merely parroted from those of his wife.

Anne smiled, as if to accommodate his words. "I do try, Father, but the simpering ways of most young ladies of my acquaintance bore me to distraction,'' she exclaimed, not taking his remarks or her answers too seriously. They had been uttered all too frequently. She helped herself to the tempting food set upon the heavy, carved sideboard. Squire Marshall set a good table.

Quentin watched his remarkable daughter a moment. No beauty, but truly a handsome woman, he thought. He took great pride in her ability to ride and hunt. He had taught her those skills since she could first sit a saddle. Having no son, he had encouraged these pursuits himself to the vocal dismay of his wife, Caroline. She now haunted him with what she perceived as Annemarie's "unnatural pursuits" and clearly placed these "detracting attributes" at his doorstep.

Caroline had chided on more occasions than he cared to remember: "How will she find a husband if she continues to excel in unladylike endeavors generally left to men?" Quentin was inordinately proud of his daughter but saw her acknowledged difference, if not the common demeanor for a lady, infinitely more interesting.

As for a husband, he secretly smiled. He had the means to make a match his wife would delight in, and he would use that power to bring it about.

While Quentin mused over his perceived attributes of his daughter, Caroline Marshall entered the room with a regal bearing that was remarkable in its effect, for she was short and rotund. Years of reminding anyone within listening distance that she was a baron's daughter attributed to the bearing that reflected her thoughts of self-consequence.

After all, she had brought Sutton Hall and its lands to the marriage along with a rather sizable dowry. This fact, of course, added to her sense of superiority, since Quentin had received only a small inheritance from his mother. Those properties had long been sold off on some speculative venture or other and Caroline was never sure whether they had been successful or not. Quentin Marshall controlled her money and kept the knowledge of the results of his investments in complete secrecy. It was suspect that the secrecy concealed a general lack of much success, for Quentin's nature would have compelled his vaunted show of any gain.

From time to time Caroline had been compelled to practice "small economies," and those intervals seemed, of late, to come with greater frequency. She silently deplored his pursuit into commerce, for gentry and noble gentlemen did not deal in anything so common. This added to the hidden belief that she was socially better than her husband. She regretted occasionally having permitted this handsome man to turn her head so that she had rushed headlong into her marriage. She would see that Annemarie did not make the same mistake and spend her life counting pennies.

Seldom did Caroline allow her opinions to go unmarked, but this was one area in which she wisely and silently refrained from any comment. She shivered as she remembered the violent rage her husband had displayed early in their marriage when she had actually questioned the wisdom of his actions. Mrs. Marshall never again ventured into that realm of conversation. All these thoughts were well schooled in a hidden, detached expression.

"Good morning," Caroline said, adjusting her gown gracefully about her feet, as she took her place at the end of the table. "Just some tea and rolls," she directed the servant with a floating wave of short, stubby fingers.

Anne smiled, for she knew bonbons would later undo the attempt her mother made to whittle her waist.

"Quentin, I have decided that we must take Annemarie to London for the little Season. I know she did not 'take' precisely on her come-out, but there were two proposals Annemarie rejected." She frowned at this memory and cast an accusative glance toward her daughter. "It is almost too late to find her a husband. Twenty-two is practically on the shelf, so we must settle her before it is beyond possibility."

Anne's hand paused in midair with a sliver of ham dangling on her fork. Her heart sank. She glanced to her father in apprehension, hopeful support, or both.

"I've put out that money already. It's far too costly . . . gowns, balls and all," he replied tersely.

"Quentin, we're invited to stay at my brother's house. We do not have to provide a ball. It will only cost the necessary gowns," Caroline replied, her small blue eyes darting from daughter to husband.

"Mother, you know I am not at all the town beauty, and the effort and expense will be wasted. I cannot abide the dandified gentlemen that abound in London and will accept none," Anne countered.

"Annemarie, you continually vex me! You will do as your father and I wish, for you must be settled."

Sitting back in his chair, Quentin placed his napkin upon the table and began to rise. "I will think about this and inform you of my decision."

Watching her father take his leave, Anne longed to escape, for she realized she was about to be presented with another lecture on her duty to marry—and marry as well as possible.

"I do not suit the unending silly pursuits of the *ton*, Mother, and well you know it," Anne stated.

"All too well. But that is partly because of your attitude.

What man wants to dance with a partner who discusses riding and hunting! Men prefer a woman to be more feminine. They can discuss riding with their male counterparts. With a woman they want charm,'' she chided.

"Mother, I'm not charming!''

"Indeed, you're far too blunt,'' Mrs. Marshall replied, her face flushing as she rolled her eyes to heaven as if to seek deliverance.

"I'm too tall and simply cannot manage missish airs. Can you imagine a woman who is seven inches over five feet simpering? It's laughable. I'm simply not able to carry off such behavior,'' Anne said.

Caroline stared at her daughter, unable to refute the truth of her words.

"Surely you do not forget my last, rather scandalous behavior in the response to Lord Rottingham's disgusting interest,'' Anne persisted.

"You exasperate me beyond measure. That unfortunate episode will have been forgotten. To London we will go and a husband you will have,'' Mrs. Marshall said, her lace cap slightly askew as she rose red-faced and angry. She left the room, her self-assumed dignity rather frayed.

With a sinking heart, Anne also rose from the table and allowed the most dejected thoughts to run through her mind. Remembering all too well her previous Season, she frowned with fierce distaste. Of course, she admitted, she had been younger and very shy in the ballroom. It was on the riding field or the estate where she could be herself.

All too well she remembered the numerous dances when she sat unasked. There were a few who sought her out, but she seemed to attract gentlemen who could not take their eyes off her well-rounded figure no matter how modest her gown. She had hated their silky compliments and the hidden meaning in their eyes. Anne shuddered at the thought.

Entering the walled garden ablaze with asters, chrysanthemums, and late roses, she seated herself upon a stone bench and folded her hands. This demure picture belied the remembered night of Lady Sutherland's ball and the incident that had abruptly ended her social Season, sending her packing back to Sutton Hall. Anne smiled to herself. What had once been a social disaster now amused her.

That fateful night Lord Rottingham, a handsome rake, led Annemarie onto the dance floor. He had not missed the voluptuous figure under the simple white gown. Using his considerable charm, he brought laughter to her lips and a sparkle to her exceptional hazel eyes. She is striking, he thought, and her womanly body set his blood on fire. This was no exceptional tribute to Miss Marshall, as that state of his blood seemed to be his general manner. Although slightly in his cups, he cleverly put her at ease and without her notice maneuvered her into a secluded alcove. Previously he had used disguised and practiced charm to lower her defenses, but the liquor he had consumed now caused him to drop his calculated manner. He then mistakenly made an obvious, ungentlemanly request as he slipped his hand from her shoulder toward her enticing, high-rounded breast.

At the precise moment Lord Rottingham was pursuing his favorite indoor pastime with Miss Marshall, the resplendent, corpulent Prince of Wales sauntered into the ballroom, surrounded by his devoted entourage. The Prince of Wales graciously made his way through, greeting the assembled guests. He had bowed over Lady Jersey's extended hand just as a high-pitched squeal echoed through the entire ballroom.

From the alcove Annemarie had raised her voice in an affronted bellow. Placing a firm hand on Lord Rottingham's chest, she backed him up with a tongue lashing that included language heard only in such places as stables and naval yards. This was shocking, for certainly it was no language that would ever cross the pink ears of a delicately raised young lady.

As Lord Rottingham struggled to gain control of the hysterical chit, he continued backing up while desperately trying to shush the shrew. His retreat was abruptly halted as he backed into the elegant Lady Jersey, who was then propelled into the Prince Regent's corpulent, decorated chest.

While it was later confirmed that the Prince had not actually been knocked down, which could only have been attributed to the swift actions of his cronies, the Prince, nevertheless, had not been amused.

A hush had fallen over the room. Annemarie stood scarlet-faced with hands clenched as Lord Rottingham effusively bowed, muttering profound apologies to the Prince. Prinny stood slightly shaken and pale while Lady Jersey adjusted her plumed turban. Rottingham continued bowing and made a hasty departure.

To his never-to-be-forgotten horror, Rottingham's retreat was to the resounding words, ''And don't you ever lay a hand on me again!''

The scandal delighted the *ton*. Miss Marshall was dubbed the Warrior Maiden, and Beau Brummell was said to have remarked, ''The realm has a second Boadicea.''

Mrs. Marshall had been aghast but kept her counsel until they had arrived home, whereupon she burst into raging tears.

Quentin Marshall was secretly delighted at his daughter's firm handling of the situation and stated that he could not see why his wife was so distraught.

''Quentin, surely you see she has disgraced herself. Rottingham is a powerful man and he will ruin her reputation. She should have discreetly and firmly put him in his place without the whole polite world as witness,'' Caroline Marshall wailed. ''Including the Prince of Wales!''

"Polite world? Mother, he insulted me," Anne interjected.

"Anne, leave me. You have disgraced me. They will think I have raised a hoyden, and I fear it is so. I won't be able to show my face again," her mother cried in self-pity with no real concern for the insult her daughter had received.

Sitting in the solace of the lovely garden, Anne smiled in remembrance, for no single action had given her more pleasure. She had unmasked to the world just what a cad Lord Rottingham was, and she had inadvertently achieved her wish to leave London. Her mother had promptly returned the family to Sutton Hall.

Anne was blissfully unaware that she had earned an enemy and that Lord Rottingham had casually let it be known that Miss Marshall was a tease.

3

The journey to London gave Seth time to define and carefully set his initial plans. Agreeing with his mother on the vindication his father's name, he held little interest in his father's family and none in the inheritance. Yet, there was a nagging curiosity, and the wish to know if his grandfather was alive. He decided to be cautious. He simply could not knock on their door and announce himself.

First, they stayed in an inn that allowed Seth time to scout London and judge appropriate locations in which to live. Both men were astounded by the teeming city. Drays, carriages, and vehicles of every description choked the streets. Hawkers cried their wares, darting without fear among the congested traffic. The city was exciting and alive with the vigorous activity of its swarming inhabitants.

They observed the gray squalor and pitiful plight of many wretched inhabitants and the contrasting broad elegant streets of the West End. This overwhelming difference took them by surprise and left them both uneasy.

America had its poor and wretched, but not on such a sweeping scale, nor were the rich of America living in the grand manner that was apparent by the elegant mansions and finely dressed aristocrats.

It became obvious they needed to improve their rustic

wardrobe. Angus and Seth were amazed that they attracted mocking attention with their poorly tailored coats.

"You've got to admit, Seth, our clothes do look countrified next to these dandy English fellows," Angus remarked, much to Seth's total amusement.

"Angus, you amaze me! I didn't think I'd see the day you'd make such an observation," Seth said with a broad and devilish grin.

Angus blushed.

"We'll visit Weston. I've learned he is the one to outfit a proper English gentleman," Seth said.

"Yep, but you'll not make an English dandy out of a Scot-American. My ancestors would rise from the Highlands to smite me."

Seth laughed. "I have no intention of becoming a coxcomb. We'll do what is necessary to be acceptable. I'd love to see one of these fellows trekking the wilderness."

"Boggles the mind," Angus said, watching a tulip of the first stare pass by in a purple coat, buttercup-yellow waistcoat, and collar points so high they completely prohibited head movement. Angus glanced at Seth and raised an eyebrow in utter disbelief.

Seth chuckled. "Your point is well taken."

It was a soberly dressed man in a dark-brown superfine cloth coat, fitted to perfection, who called on the solicitor whose name appeared on some of his father's papers.

James Addison was getting on in years and no longer spending the long hours practicing law as he once had. His body seemed, these days, to resist much exertion and his interest was also slowly waning. He left much of the work to his two capable sons.

There were several accounts in which he still held interest, including that of old Lord Blakewell, the Earl of Chathram. In fact, he greatly admired the old gentleman.

A frown crossed his thin, lined face whenever he thought of Cecil Blakewell and his ne'er-do-well son, Anthony. It was a tragedy, that the older son, John, had killed a man and later died at sea while fleeing England. John seemed to be a fine young man. Well, Addison mused, one could never truly know what is in the heart or character of a man. Besides, he hadn't thought of young John in years . . .

The old solicitor's curiosity had been peaked upon receiving a letter requesting an interview from a Mr. Blakewell. The request raised a vague premonition. The name was merely a coincidence, he was sure, but he agreed to meet the gentleman.

Entering the barrister's comfortable-looking office, Seth introduced himself. "I am Seth Blakewell of Savannah, Georgia, and wish to extend my appreciation in your accommodation to see me."

James Addison glanced up to the man with the timbered voice who had just completed what amounted to a small speech. He was a man of few words himself, but rose to extend his hand. He carefully scrutinized the tall, rugged man before him. Mr. Addison perceived that the soberly dressed man was confident and purposeful, yet he detected a slight nervousness. He observed that the athletic build and the color of Blakewell's skin indicated an outdoor existence. An eerie curiosity tinged with foreboding crept up his spine when he noted the signet ring on Mr. Blakewell's finger.

"Be seated, young man. How may I be of service to you?" he asked, almost afraid to hear the answer.

Seth sat a moment taking in the measure of the frail bespectacled man before him, and wondered where to begin.

"I am the son of the late John Blakewell. You may have

known him, for I have his papers and your name appears on a few of them. My purpose in coming to England is to clear his name of a crime he did not commit. I also want to know if my grandfather is still alive and, if so, to meet him," Seth said, carefully noting the reaction of the barrister.

Astonished, James Addison took a small gasp of air and paused to mull over this information. Surprise first showed on his wizened face, quickly replaced by a more cynical expression. He had been a barrister far too long to assume a man's intent was honorable.

Nervously removing a handkerchief from his pocket, Addison slowly rubbed the lenses of his spectacles. Silence and time seemed to hang suspended. A muscle moved in the stoic American's jaw.

"That is your only objective?" Mr. Addison finally asked, leveling a speculative gaze at the gentleman.

"It is," Seth replied.

"You do not intend to petition the courts or your grandfather for what, if what you tell me is true, would be the right of the heir to the Earl of Chathram?" Addison asked suspiciously.

"I have no such intention at this time," Seth answered.

A glimmer of doubt hovered in the back of Addison's mind. "I find it hard to believe you would stir up these matters for any intention other than financial gain."

"It is your right to believe as you wish. I am a very wealthy man and do not need to acquire the title or monies that belong to my grandfather. I take it by your reply, he is, in fact, still living," Seth said.

"He is. And if what you claim is true, he will take it grievously that your father lived through the journey and never contacted him. It nearly killed him when the shooting took place—over cards no less—forcing his elder son to flee.''

"Ah, but he never knew that my father was innocent. Father assumed the blame in order to protect his younger brother, Cecil. It is my heritage and my mother's wish that his name be cleared,'' Seth said, his voice carrying an incisive edge.

Mr. Addison surveyed the American gentleman a moment. "You have proof of such allegations?'' he asked.

"I cannot prove what happened on that fateful night. However, I will relate what my father told my mother, and I have his documents, signet ring, and the purse of gold Cecil paid the captain of the ship to see to his brother's demise.''

The small, stuffy room seemed to grow warmer and oppressive as Seth told the story of his uncle's betrayal. James Addison listened with growing apprehension. If these events were true and the man before him was bent on seeking the earldom, the scandal would ruin the family and probably kill the aging Lord Blakewell.

James Addison examined the documents without comment. He then raised his eyes to Mr. Blakewell. "What do you want of me? I contemplate nothing but scandal and heartache if this matter is pursued.''

"This matter does not need to be made public. I want you to arrange a meeting with my grandfather. I should also like information about my Uncle Cecil,'' Seth replied.

"I'm not sure I will agree to mediate in this matter,'' James Addison said. "I must consider it carefully.''

"I understand, but keep in mind I can make such arrangements myself.''

Mr. Addison looked into those strange green-gray eyes and realized the gentleman was making no threat, only stating a fact.

"Cecil spends his time at Chathram Manor, which has not prospered under his management. He gambled much away in his youth, and I fear his son Anthony now spends most evenings emulating his father," Mr. Addison said, giving the truthful information in the hopes of putting off this determined American—if, in fact, he was after some monetary gain.

Seth seized upon his statement. "Does my cousin Anthony owe many gambling debts?"

With a sinking heart, for perhaps he had revealed too much, Mr. Addison nodded.

"Buy them up," Seth said.

"Buy up all his vowels?" Addison asked.

"Yes, all, but do it discreetly without anyone knowing who is behind it. Let them assume it is the Earl of Chathram," Seth instructed. "Well, for now I think our business is concluded. Arrange the meeting at Chathram Manor with my grandfather, that is all else I require."

Seth rose, gathered up the papers, and carefully wrapped them into the leather pouch.

"I am at a loss of what to believe," James Addison said.

Seth's expression hardened. "In America, sir, a man's word is his honor."

"Well, yes, of course . . . but you must understand my position. I must weigh this matter," James Addison replied with a worried frown on his shocked face. "In England also, Mr. Blakewell, a gentleman's word is considered his honor."

Seth met the old gentleman's eyes and nodded approval. "I expect our transaction to remain confidential, Mr. Addison," Seth said.

"But of course. This is my duty," Addison said.

They parted with the understanding that Mr. Addison would consider making the arrangements for a visit to the Earl of Chathram.

Seth left the offices in the narrow building. Placing his hat on his head, he frowned. While he had expected just such a reaction, he was nevertheless annoyed by the fact that his story had been doubted. Yet, he believed Mr. Addison did not totally disregard its possible truth. That would have to do for now. Seth had meant to seek his advice on appropriate housing, but the conversation had not gone that far.

Setting the interview aside, and accompanied by Angus, Seth set out to accomplish their other tasks. They ordered a fine carriage and smart phaeton. Angus was completely taken with the phaeton, for he had never seen one before coming to England. Delighted as a young boy with a new pony and cart, Angus walked around the vehicle, eyeing the large spoked wheels.

"It seems as though they are all the crack, as the English would say." Seth chuckled. "I'm afraid I'll feel more than a little silly perched up so high, but we must follow the dictates of fashion, since it seems absolutely necessary if we are to breach the bastions of society."

Angus laughed. "We've come a long way, and I'm not sure where we are."

A grave expression crossed Seth's face and he shrugged. "Neither am I. We know for a fact we'll be two well-dressed fools perched atop a newfangled carriage without the foggiest of where we're going."

"But if I know you, we'll get there," Angus said with a chuckle.

A smile lit Seth's eyes and face. He nodded.

Tatterstall's, near Hyde Park Turnpike, was the popular place to purchase horses. There were stables, loose boxes, and a large circular arena, all enclosed for the purpose of trying out horses. The Jockey Club was the center for the well-known racing fraternity and the hub concerning turf betting.

It is not surprising, therefore, when purchasing the needed horses that the two Americans met Lord Charling.

Angus was inspecting the fine animals and helping Seth in their selection. It was during their discussion that Lord Charling introduced himself.

"If I may be of assistance, please allow me," Lord Charling volunteered. "At least I can help in what would be a fair price. It is obvious you are new to our shores, and though I should not like to admit it, it might be considered great sport to fleece two Americans. I am Lord Harley Charling, at your service," he said with a slight nod.

Seth eyed the impeccably dressed aristocrat and seized the opportunity to speak with him. If Addison failed him, he would need a means of introduction into the *ton*. He wanted to meet Cecil on equal ground. Why else would he be going through all this damn rigmarole? he mused while extending his hand to Charling.

"Seth Blakewell, sir, and my friend Angus Grey. We are most obliged, sir. I have found what I consider excellent animals for my equipage, and would be very appreciative of your opinion. However, we are both eager to find some outstanding mounts," Seth said.

"Well, if that is the circumstance, I greatly recommend seeing Quentin Marshall of Surrey. He raises the finest horses in England," Lord Charling said, deliberately failing to mention it was rumored that Squire Marshall's daughter engaged in this unladylike venture. It was something a gentleman would choose to ignore and not repeat.

Blakewell stiffened and cast a sharp glance toward Angus, who shifted in response. Neither spoke for a moment.

"I'll take that under advisement," Seth finally said in an even voice, his black brows rising over eyes as sharp as an eagle's spotting prey.

Lord Charling continued to converse in a congenial manner, offering to show them about town.

"Least I can do," Charling said as he took his leave.

The remark escaped both Seth and Angus, but they agreed to his offer.

"Why should he feel obligated to carry us about?" asked Angus.

"Damn if I know, but it suits our mission," Seth replied.

"Do you have the feeling you've just been doing business with a Yankee trader?" Angus shrewdly asked.

"You've a keen eye, you rogue," Seth said, and they laughed together with the confidence of men who could take care of themselves.

It was through this chance meeting and Charling's ready invitation that Seth and Angus found their way into a discreet gaming house in St. James's Street, where the size of one's purse was perhaps more important than social connections. Charling had used the opportunity to escort the two new-comers in experiencing the many "interesting" aspects of London's nightlife.

Although an aristocrat, Lord Charling was an ivory-turner known for luring novices and innocents into London gaming hells in order to fleece them. Impeccably dressed at all times, he was born a true wit and an insatiable gambler. Lord Charling was more than a gamester; he was a sharper. With the apparent ease of pleasing and the refined accomplishments of a gentleman, he suggested a friendly game.

Charling easily drew Seth into play. He was not exceptionally clever, or he might have realized it had been accomplished with far too much facility. As with most sharpers, he began by handling the cards awkwardly, rather like a bungler.

He advanced his bets by degrees, keeping his opponents in good spirits with insignificant winnings, thereby giving no show of all his skill. To do so would send an opponent to flight, and above all, Charling disguised his increase in advantage amid conversations of estate, honor, and whatever else would be diverting.

Well aware of Charling's tactics, Seth used the opportunity to inform Lord Charling—and everyone within hearing distance—that he was a plantation-owner from America. Hoping to have the information well-known, he went on to mention the three ships he owned that plied the seas to the West Indies, making huge profits during the Embargo Act and the Non-intercourse Act previously enacted by the American congress.

Seth was well aware that these measures had created outrage in both England and America. Knowledge of his running of the blockades to trade might not hurt his status in English opinion, since he had paid the enormous import fees and brought much-needed cotton to English industry. Perhaps, while not creating amiable feelings toward Americans, he at least might not cause hostility.

"Indeed," the interested Lord Charling dryly commented as his slender white fingers drew in his winnings. The evening had great promise, Lord Charling thought, pleased with his change of fortune. Seth smiled, showing a seemingly innocent expression.

"So it is trade that brings you to London?" Lord Charling asked in cheerful distraction as he fleetly and neatly stacked his chips.

"Yes, always said a man can't make too much money. I'm looking for favorable investments," Seth loudly said, knowing his crass remarks would earn him disdain from the other assembled aristocrats. It did. Only an American would

speak so coarsely, several elegant gentlemen thought.
Let Lord Charling fleece the brash American well, all
agreed.

Angus, no gambler, meanwhile circled the room, tasting
the various dishes set out for the players and surveying the
minutiae of every member and all proceedings. His eye was
as keen as Seth's. Living on a frontier, sometimes with
Indians, gave a man a sharp edge in observation.

At the evening's end, which was indeed a misnomer, for
the sky was pale pink in the east, they left the gaming house.
Seth had dropped several hundred pounds, knowing full well
that Lord Charling had deliberately allowed him to win on
a number of occasions.

"Why are you smiling like a jester? You lost, Seth,
and no wee amount," Angus chided. "You disappointed
me."

"Ah, but we now have our entry, for Lord Charling, in
his eagerness to acquire our friendship to fatten his purse,
has graciously offered to introduce us about. The honor is
dubious, be assured. I also learned Lord Kenworth lost a
fortune only a few nights ago and is almost ruined. That
information is worth the money I lost! Besides, Lord Charling
thinks he is drawing me in for a much bigger prize."

"That's easy enough to understand; he has a flunky who
stands at the mirror over the mantel to signal what his
opponent holds," Angus said derisively. "I tried to signal
you, but you'd pay me no mind."

"Is that how he does it? You see, I do need you to keep
me from harm's way," he said.

"I'll not be nursemaid to you again. Best you beware,"
Angus warned.

Seth halted his steps. "Angus, you know I am no gambler,
but it was necessary to learn all that I have in this evening's

work. Incidentally, they wondered why you didn't gamble. I told them you were a Methodist.''

"How did you explain the champagne I drank?" Angus asked with delight.

"I didn't," Seth replied, and they both continued down the street laughing. "In their view, there's no explaining Americans, I'm sure."

With the information gleaned during the previous evening's play, Seth moved with dispatch. A man of great talent and astute business ability, he proceeded immediately to establish them by leasing a very handsome villa in Portland Place from the financially desperate Lord Kenworth. Upon hearing of this gentleman's loss of thirty thousand pounds in one evening's gambling, Seth had presented himself to the nobleman with the offer to lease the house and its servants at a price that was swiftly accepted. Lord Kenworth promptly retired to the country.

Events are moving nicely, Seth thought. They had the correct address and an entry into society, however dubious. He perceived Lord Charling was considered a dangerous man, even if he were an impoverished viscount.

Seth wisely used his time awaiting Mr. Addison's reply to learn all he could about the business community, returning again and again to the docks. He saw the West India Docks and the congestion in the Thames with ships lying off the Legal Quays. It was apparent many ships were forced to wait in midstream, even for weeks, for lighters to unload them. Often he saw them queued up, three and four abreast, all the way up the river from Woolwich. There's money to be made here, he thought. He had learned the monies going into the building of the much-needed docks were from private investments. He would make his interest in such investments known.

* * *

There was little to occupy Cecil, so he often pried among his father's records. He opened the sealed missive from Mr. Addison with the intention of resealing it before he gave it to his father. It was a trick he used often, figuring it was his right to know all that pertained to the earldom. Reading the letter, Cecil panicked at the news of a possible son to his older brother. He trembled as he read Addison's letter, which he swiftly destroyed with little thought to any possible following request. He quickly wrote a terse refusal to Mr. Addison, thinking to end the inquiry. What he had buried so long ago now presented a devastating threat, and he knew he must find a way to deal with it.

A week later Mr. Addison sent a note to Seth informing him that the Earl of Chathram would not receive him. Both were unaware that it was Cecil who had secretly issued the refusal.

Seth read Addison's reply with a flood of mixed feelings. He had failed in having his grandfather agree to meet with him, and he realized suddenly that it meant a great deal to him. However, he paused, for the reality of the warning Mr. Addison had made on the heartache of such past dealings brought him no joy. He ran his hand through his black hair and frowned. Crumpling the letter, he tossed it into the fire and stood watching it flame up then die in hues of blue and gold flames. Perhaps it was best, although he knew deep down he could not permit it to end with this refusal.

Seth had been spending the past weeks making arrangements in the event of just such a refusal. He would proceed with his plans, and the devil take all. He was a man who held no physical fear. Having hunted in the wildest country and spent time among the Creeks, he had also risked life and limb slipping the blockade to reap huge profits, and he now stood filled with trepidation. Where would all this lead?

4

Quentin Marshall greeted Lord Charling with a false affability. Though he was not personally acquainted with Charling, he was very much aware of his dubious reputation.

"Good day to you," he said, extending his hand to the slender dandy.

"Squire Marshall, allow me to present to you two gentlemen from America," Lord Charling drawled. "Mr. Seth Blakewell and Mr. Angus Grey, both visitors to our shores from Savannah, Georgia. They are most desirous of seeing your fine horses. We hope our arriving unannounced does not prove an inconvenience to you." By his hauteur, it could be easily understood that Charling cared little if any inconvenience, in fact, did exist.

"Not at all, Lord Charling, you're welcome. You'll find our horses the best in all of England. Come, gentlemen, this way, please. They're exercising some beauties in the southern pasture." Quentin motioned for the three men to follow him.

Seth carefully appraised the accomplice in his father's betrayal. He saw a smiling, self-satisfied man, and resentment surged through Seth's body. Clenching his fist, he held back an overwhelming desire to beat the man senseless. He quickly subdued his impulsive reaction and allowed a thin smile to appear on his stony face. His eyes glittered with malice.

Angus gave Seth an elbow in his side as they moved in Marshall's wake. The action brought Seth up sharply, and he nodded in gratitude to his friend. I must avoid such an unguarded reaction, Seth thought, annoyed with himself.

It was a feeling first. Anne became consciously aware of being observed. Sitting astride a beautiful chestnut, she had been concentrating on the riding merits of the animal. Glancing up, she could see her father gesturing while talking with three men, who were obviously interested in the horse she was riding. Silently she cursed her riding garb, feeling a sinking pang of discomfort, for she had not thought to be interrupted.

Smiling broadly, Squire Marshall motioned her to come to them. By his manner he was extolling the excellence of his horses in hopes of a sale.

Seth leaned against the fence, watching the young woman put the magnificent chestnut through difficult paces while handling the horse with perfection. His eyes narrowed as the lady drew nearer and his focus changed suddenly, from the horse to the rider.

Recognizing Lord Charling as she drew up, she coolly nodded to him. Anne's eyes traveled to the tall, dark gentleman at his side and she tentatively smiled into his unusual eyes. He was studying her with open interest. Her cheeks grew pink under the scrutiny, and she turned her gaze away. As if to dispel the awkward moment, she quickly dismounted and led the horse to within feet of where they stood.

Seth was totally absorbed by the striking beauty of this marvelous woman. Her close-fitting breeches allowed a glimpse of her well-proportioned body. His eyes lingered on her shapely hips and slender legs, then slowly traveled up to the rounded breasts that pressed against her loose cream cambric shirt. The sun reflected shafts of gold in the tawny hair, and when she raised her hazel eyes to his, it was almost like a slap in the face. The impact was sudden, unexpected, and momentarily stunning; voices swirled around him, but he heard nothing. He was being introduced, he realized, and he brought his attention to the conversation.

Squire Marshall was making the introductions and she nodded an acknowledgment to each gentleman in turn.

Americans, she thought, that is the difference. Lord Charling was plainly shocked by her attire, for she could unmistakably see his disapproval. The tall Mr. Blakewell's interest had nothing remotely connected to the propriety of her dress. It was blatantly bold, and the intensity of his gaze made her feel vulnerable. Her mother was correct: such dress only invited undesired attention. Not knowing if she were annoyed at the bold visitor's gaze or her own choice of dress, she frowned.

"Annemarie, these gentlemen are interested in purchasing two of our fine horses as riding mounts," Quentin explained.

"I'm returning to the stables, so follow me, gentlemen, and I'll introduce you to Mr. McGuire. You'll find we have many exceptional mounts . . ." Anne's voice trailed off as she took Comet's reins and led him along the fence toward the stable. Still aware of her attire, she felt exposed and awkward. Mr. Blakewell's gaze seemed to burn on her back. Turning suddenly, she asked, "Mr. Blakewell, are you related to the family of the Earl of Chathram?"

"I'm an American, Miss Marshall," he replied.

"Merely a coincidence, my dear," Quentin quickly answered, but his skin took on a slight ashen hue. He had previously noticed the magnificent ring on Mr. Blakewell's finger and the two thoughts connected into a vague fear.

Upon reaching the stables, Anne gave instructions to one of the stable boys to take Comet and brush her down. She started to make her excuses to leave when Lord Charling espied Taliesin.

"What an Irish hunter! He's magnificent," he exclaimed. "And just what price is he?"

"My lord, he is not for sale," she said.

"I'm afraid he is my daughter's, and part with him she would not." Squire Marshall beamed with pride. The animal lent a substantial air to the quality of the animals within their stables.

Seth stepped forward and raised his hand to touch Taliesin's nose. The animal snorted, shook his head, and backed away.

"He is a mighty beast. Far too much for a woman," Seth said.

Anne's head turned sharply and her eyes widened. "He's not too much for me. In fact, he will answer to no one but me," she stated as she moved beside Seth and coaxed Taliesin to her. The great black hunter nuzzled Anne when she placed her cheek along the horse's, cooing sweet words.

Seth stood quietly and watched them. He studied her face. Not beautiful, he thought, but totally captivating. She had a slender nose, almond eyes, and full, expressive mouth over even white teeth. He was astonished by the flashes of gold and green when she raised her eyes to his and smiled.

"Taliesin is the finest horse I've ever owned. And as with Irish hunters, he has one master," she boasted.

"Perhaps one day he'll let me ride him," Seth said.

"It's not likely. Now, you all must excuse me. I'll leave you to your business," she said as she moved to leave.

"Tell your mother we have three guests for luncheon," Quentin Marshall called to her as she passed through the stable door.

She paused and nodded, her tall frame silhouetted against the light passing through the door.

Seth stood a moment watching the empty space, and when he turned, he saw Angus' eyes resting speculatively on him. Angus cocked an eyebrow and smiled, his merry eyes dancing. He had been silent during the whole encounter, had missed nothing, and was vastly amused. Seth returned the smile and let out a soft whistle as he shifted to look at the empty doorway.

The men took up the business at hand. Seth had a hard time bringing his attention to the various merits of the horses, and he allowed Angus to take the lead in the choices. Angus was delighted, taking a keen interest in any possible selection Mr. McGuire showed.

Anne informed her mother that they would be having guests for luncheon. She had not changed her riding attire and, as expected, was firmly censured by her mother.

"Mother, it makes no difference. They are here to purchase horses. I shall appear properly dressed for the noon meal, I assure you."

"Lord Charling, certainly a rather unsavory character, is a gossip of the first order. Annemarie, you must put aside those unappropriate clothes once and for all."

"I had not expected company, Mother. I wear them solely while working with the horses," Anne argued, weary of the topic.

" 'Tis simply not fitting! I will no longer tolerate it," Caroline wailed.

"You have to admit we need the money the horses bring in. It is Mr. McGuire and I who create that income, and it would be near impossible to do so on sidesaddle."

Mrs. Marshall had no time to reply, for Annemarie quickly left the room. To her chagrin, Caroline realized the words her daughter spoke were true. Times were not easy now, or so it seemed from the economies that Mr. Marshall was insisting upon. She shook her head and decided to say no more for the present. Smoothing her dress and straightening her lace morning cap, Mrs. Marshall went to seek the cook to arrange a menu for the guests.

Anne climbed the stairway of the comfortable family manor. The house was old, with many additions, nooks, and crannies giving it a solid atmosphere. The walls were paneled in most rooms and the wood glowed with mellow aging and constant care.

She loved the house, and as she entered her room, she cast a quick, appreciative glance. Her bed dressings were made of a beautiful indienne print in colors of burgundy, gold, and green, all fading to a soft mellow harmony against the rich oiled woods. The room was situated on the southeast corner, so it received the morning light and lingering winter sun. The two windows set in alcoves with diamond-shaped leaded panes boasted window seats. She had spent many hours on those seats dreaming of adventures one might find in far corners of the world.

Anne remembered that once she wished she had been a man and could go off to India. This was at the time her father was discussing the possibilities of financial ventures in India. But the conversation, like her dreams, had eventually faded.

Smiling at Flora, who was busy fussing about, Anne crossed the room to her large, carved wardrobe. With a quick flourish she pulled out her green muslin dress. Handing it to Flora, she said, "I'll wear this for luncheon. We're to have company."

Flora looked a bit surprised. "It becomes you, Miss Anne," she added with a hint of interest in her voice.

A bath was prepared to rid her of the "horse smell," as

her mother had so often remarked, wrinkling her nose in distaste.

Annemarie took down her hair and ran her fingers through it as she gazed at her reflection in the mirror, turning her head one way, then another as she examined her features. A soft sigh escaped her lips; she wished she was pretty.

Turning away from the mirror and its disappointing reflection with a shrug, she began to remove her riding clothes. Stepping into the delightfully warm water, she added a revealing thought: "Flora, I wish to look my best today, so I'm putting myself in your capable hands."

Flora nodded with interest.

Some time later, Flora beamed with pride and eagerly began to dress her mistress's beautiful hair. This time she used all the skill she had long wished to display, and the results could be considered nothing but charming. Shiny tendrils framed Anne's face, and the carefully coiffed arrangement gave the appearance of casual tumbling curls. The style enhanced her excellent bone structure and elegant neck. Annemarie did not consider herself pretty, and that thought had been often reinforced by her mother's remarks.

Annemarie gasped a moment and turned to Flora. "It changes me. It looks wonderful."

"If you'd listened to me before, you'd have seen what I've been saying all along," Flora replied with puffed-up pride.

Annemarie laughed. "I shall be your humble subject, I vow, when we wish to set our best example."

"And just who is it for that you wish to set such a fine appearance, I wonder?" Flora questioned with a teasing grin.

"You're impertinent," Anne said, smiling in return.

Flora dropped a curtsy. "Aye, Miss Anne, I am." But only humor shone from her eyes.

Anne took one last look of appraisal. The pleated dress

had an overskirt of muslin. The bodice crossed in pleats that softly molded her figure. The puffed sleeves were also pleated and gave a slight, tailored effect, rather than appearing fussy. Frills would never suit her statuesque figure. This time Anne smiled in approval, and a soft glow of pink heightened her high cheekbones.

Seth was seated next to Squire Marshall when Miss Marshall entered the room with her mother. He rose at their entrance and watched her gracefully cross the room. What a magnificent woman, he thought. His hooded eyes traveled the length of her elegant figure, and he felt a slight tremor reverberate through his body.

"What a delightful surprise to have you join us for luncheon," Mrs. Marshall gushed as the introductions were made. "Imagine, all the way from America. My, my, you must have tales to tell, all about wild Indians and such . . ."

Angus smiled at Seth. "Yes, indeed, and the thing about it is, you never know when you might meet up with one."

Seth's grey-green eyes sparkled a split second. "And you can never be too careful at the possibility of such an encounter," he added.

"Heavens, I imagine so. I should faint quite dead away if I ever encountered one."

Seth changed his attention to Anne. "And how would you manage such a frightful event, Miss Marshall?" His low, resonant voice carried a caressing quality.

Anne felt the power of this man invade her body. She paused a moment. Even as tall as she was, she had to raise her eyes to his when she replied. "Why, I should certainly appraise the situation before I fainted dead away."

Seth nodded his approval.

Anne returned his gaze. He was a compelling man. Caution would have to be her shield, she knew instantly.

To Anne's relief, Mrs. Jacobs announced luncheon was ready to be served.

Lord Charling, because of his rank, was seated to the right of Mrs. Marshall. Seth Blackwell was seated next to Lord Charling and to the left of Squire Marshall, who had hopes of consummating the purchase of his two horses. Annemarie sat to the right of her father, beside Angus Grey.

Annemarie wondered how soon it would be before her mother informed their guests she was a baron's daughter. She did not have to wait long.

"However do you manage in the colonies without an aristocracy to arrange things? My father, Lord Sutton, always said a society would deteriorate to chaos without the leadership of the gentry," she said as an opening topic to the meal, thereby establishing her perceived importance.

Squire Marshall hid his annoyance and Annemarie tried to hide a smile.

"We seem to manage, ma'am," Seth said.

"Opportunities are unlimited. Great wealth is to be made in the new country, if a man is capable of doing so," Angus said. "My family came from Scotland because my father is a second son, and we now own a vast holding in Georgia, as does Mr. Blakewell."

"And where are your people from, Mr. Blakewell? We have neighbors by that name, incidentally," Mrs. Marshall asked.

"My people are from England, as so many of the inhabitants of Georgia are," Seth replied. Lest the discussion stray into the obvious area of his relatives, Seth continued, "I have interests in shipping, with three of the finest and fastest ships that sail the Atlantic and Caribbean. Since we're out of Savannah, I have a distinct advantage as a privateer. We brought tobacco and cotton through the embargo blockades to the much-needed industry of England. The whole confusing tangle of laws of both countries—and France, of course—makes it most profitable. If one in three ships returns, a great profit is made. In all these years, I have lost just one ship.''

All eyes were turned to him in fascination.

"You captained your own ships?" Squire Marshall asked.

"No. I'm no sailor, but I have the finest captains and crews available," he said. Seth was satisfied with the direction of the conversation. Angus had led it nicely. He could see the interest in the Squire's eyes, and he knew the groundwork was laid. He toyed with his wineglass and a cynical expression crossed his face. When he glanced up to find Miss Marshall's eyes upon him, his resolve faltered for a moment.

Anne was fascinated by the discourse—for different reasons than her father. It was the adventurous aspects that caught her imagination.

Not so with Caroline Marshall, who frowned with disapproval. No gentleman of quality would engage in such commerce, let along brag about it. She dismissed all Americans as boors.

Lord Charling had remained unusually quiet. He was accustomed to leading nearly all conversations in the light, amusing banter so necessary for survival in the upper echelons of society.

"Do inform us of the latest gossip of London, Lord Charling, for we intend to seek the pleasures of London within a fortnight. Please bring us up to date. I fear all this talk of business is quite above me," Caroline asked with more than a little censure in her voice.

Anne dropped her eyes. Squire Marshall vowed to seek another opportunity to speak with the American when ladies were not present to interrupt. Quentin's interest in Mr. Blakewell had shifted from who he was to the possible idea of a promising commercial venture.

Seth allowed a small satisfied smile; he had accomplished what he wished. Angus sent a very speaking glance to Seth in approval. It was acknowledged with a slight nod.

Annemarie watched for a moment the dark mysterious countenance of Mr. Blakewell, and she knew instinctively he was not usually so open in his manner. There was a calculating quality of purpose about him. He met her eyes once more, and her interest was peaked.

5

A slosh of wine spilled over the edge of his glass during dinner as Quentin Marshall effusively expounded on the advantageous sale he had made to Mr. Blakewell. He was curious about the American, even though a foreboding hovered in the back of his mind. Quentin smiled smugly to himself. He could always "smell" a profit, and like many speculators, he overvalued his talents.

Caroline watched the red wine stain spread on the pristine white linen, and sent a disapproving look to her husband. He could be so boorish, she thought.

Perceiving her censure, he quickly changed the subject to placate her and, at the same time, achieve his own ends.

"My dear," Quentin said, "I am in agreement. We will go up to London. Annemarie must have another chance to meet a fine young man and settle down to a family of her own."

"I am gratified you see it as I do. Annemarie, you must not fail to secure a husband this time," Caroline said, glancing at her daughter.

Annemarie kept her eyes on her plate. "If there's one to be found," she said as a slight rise in color heightened her cheeks. The image of Mr. Blakewell flashed unbidden in her mind. This amused her, for such a thought had never occurred to her before. She turned a smile upon her mother.

"I shall certainly do my best. This time it may be easier for me . . ." Her voice trailed off.

"That's my girl." Marshall beamed and nodded to his wife.

"We'll leave at the end of the week. My brother has kindly extended the invitation whenever it would suit us," Mrs. Marshall said. "Quentin, we'll need funds for gowns suitable for the social events."

"I shall attend to it," he replied, thinking that he must call on Lord Cecil Blakewell and put to him firmly his intention for the betrothal of Lord Anthony and Annemarie. He would save considerable expense by getting that finally settled.

True to his intentions, Squire Marshall called on Lord Blakewell the following morning. Entering Chathram's great hall, Quentin was still surprised by the beauty, although he had crossed the threshold hundreds of times. The austere rustification of the exterior was a total contrast to the magnificent interior grandeur of the huge, lofty marble hall. A broad flight of white marble stairs rose to a second level beneath a curved, coffered apse along a colonnade of fluted Ionic columns of variegated alabaster. At the top of the stairway, two pilasters flanked an inner apse in which a door, set under a Roman pediment, led to the grand salon. The rise supporting the colonnade boasted a carved frieze, copied from Roman models via Desgodetzs' *Edifices antiques de Rome* of 1682. Marshall was no connoisseur of architecture, yet he never failed to feel the intended impact of the striking contrast upon entering the magnificent hall.

The thought of Annemarie installed in such a setting struck him for the first time. He smiled with pleasure and wondered why he had never thought of it precisely in that manner before.

Cecil was not particularly pleased to see his friend arrive but received him with cordiality. He ushered him into a small room off the left that was intimate and more comfortable, with its rich paneling and Shivan rugs. After ordering wine and sesame cakes, Lord Blakewell indicated with a gesture of his hand for Quentin to be seated in one of the chairs flanking the fireplace.

Seating himself opposite the squire and crossing his legs, Lord Blakewell said, "And to what do I owe the honor of this visit?"

"Our friendship goes back so far, I'm sure I need no excuse," Quentin said amicably, with a smile that did not match the calculating look in his eyes.

Cecil's eyes flickered a moment with the thought that Marshall was stupid. The knowledge of the secret that lay between them brought the equally hidden and likely animosity in knowing an evil truth about each other.

"No, of course not," Cecil drawled.

With tiny beads of perspiration emerging on his forehead, Marshall cleared his throat, leaned forward, and said, "There *is* a purpose in my coming, however. It is time for us to proceed with the promised betrothal between Anthony and Annemarie."

Cecil sat without movement or change of expression. He had known for years to expect this demand, and now that it had come, it came as a shock.

"That promise was made years ago, under stressing circumstances. Anthony is young. He is enjoying London. He is not partial to the bucolic activities. I strongly doubt Annemarie cares much for the social scene in London. She is far too interested in her horses."

"Caroline is eager for Annemarie to be settled," Marshall said as he took a sip of port. "What you say is true. But I should think you'd like to lure Anthony from the gambling tables of London, and how better to settle him down than with a good wife," Marshall curtly replied.

"Anne's dowry is hardly worth mentioning. Anthony could use a rich wife," Lord Blakewell retorted.

"But it is time Annemarie wed, and I wish to make the arrangements while the old earl still lives. It is my advantage to press now! I'm sure you will see that. It will also be to the Blakewells' advantage, for upon my death my lands would come into your family. Cecil, I'm calling in a debt you owe me for the aid I gave you to make you the Earl of Chathram when your father dies."

Cecil sat quietly a moment. "You would hold me to that after all these years?"

"You know I would. I have waited until the last moment, but it is time she is married," Marshall replied, and sat back.

A strained silence encompassed the two in a tense variance with each other. Marshall sat in aggressive silence. Lord Blakewell appeared shaken; courage had never been regarded as one of his attributes.

"I've received an inquiry from a Seth Blakewell to visit my father. I refused, of course, but it makes me worry. Supposing John . . ." Blakewell's voice broke the silence, then faded.

" 'Tis a long time ago. Best it lay buried. However, I sold two of my finest horses to a Mr. Blakewell yesterday. He wore a ruby signet ring of some sort," Marshall said, a sense of foreboding creeping up his spine.

"What did he say? What do you think he wants?" Cecil asked.

"Great heavens, how should I know? He claims to be wealthy and is looking for investments. Owns shipping interest and a plantation in Georgia."

"Did he inquire into Chathram Manor or its owners?"

"No. Only said his people were from England. Could be

just a coincidence in names. I'm sure that's the case. By the way, how did you refuse his visit without your father knowing?'' Marshall asked.

''That was no problem. I just didn't tell him of the letter from Mr. Addison. I answered it myself.''

''Dash it, Cecil! Your father is not senile or a flat. He'll go into a towering rage if he thinks you're usurping him.''

Blakewell ran his fingers along his cheek. ''Go to London. Learn what you can about him. I'll speak to Anthony about the marriage. They've known each other all their lives. I'm not sure they'll suit. Anthony is young. Still, marriage might be the making of him. I'll follow up in a fortnight or so. We'll just have to wait.''

Marshall again leaned forward. ''There will be no further mischief. We were young and irresponsible. Have to let it be.''

Cecil squinted his eyes. ''God, man, your imagination is running away with you. He's an impostor if he attempts to make a connection to this family. It is mere coincidence. I don't know why he wished to see Father, or if he will try again. But it wouldn't hurt to find out what you can about the man.''

''He's not likely to tell me anything,'' Marshall said with a shrug. ''But I'll pursue the matter.''

''And I'll have Anthony call on Annemarie when she gets to London. I'll have him begin his courtship and we'll see what happens. What of Annemarie? She seems no biddable miss,'' Lord Blakewell said.

Quentin was momentarily taken aback. ''She'll do as I say,'' he snapped. He stood reaching out to shake Lord Blakewell's hand. ''Have a deal, then?''

Lord Blakewell nodded, but a hard line marked his thin mouth.

*   *   *

Comfortably established in the Kenworth town house, Seth and Angus lingered over an excellent breakfast. Accustomed to plain fare and self-help, both gentlemen chafed with the inactivity of their luxurious surroundings. The silent-footed servants made Angus nervous. He had started more than once at the sudden appearance of a liveried servant attempting to provide a service Angus was quite capable of attending himself. Seth, no less, felt uneasy in this sybaritic mansion, and his restlessness grew into a vague feeling of frustration.

Angus had been talking incessantly about the fine Thoroughbreds purchased during their trip to Sutton Hall.

"I take back anything I've said about the English and their horses. Never seen better," he said, observing his friend, who merely nodded occasionally to his remarks. "Seth, you've had nothing on your face but a frown since we came back from Surrey."

"I've been thinking, first of my grandfather's refusal and then of the greedy Squire Marshall with his toad-eating affability. This endeavor is proving to be more difficult than I had expected. I held some naïve vision of merely introducing myself and explaining my father's innocence without going into details. With the refusal of my grandfather and that grasping fool Marshall, I find myself at odd ends. I'm Creek enough to seek justice, and if I'm not successful in that, then revenge will do."

"More like sweet revenge, I'd say. I saw you reduced to a stammering schoolboy. Couldn't take your eyes off the intriguing Miss Marshall."

"You become more imaginative each day, Angus. I hope you continue to do so, for it's going to take imagination to accomplish what I intend to do."

"Well, for now, I'm bored. Great heavens, what do people do here all day? Let's take the horses for a ride in the park. I could use some exercise," Angus said.

Seth readily agreed, and it was only a short time before the two gentlemen were making their way through the streets and entering Hyde Park.

They were the epitome of the fashionable English gentlemen. Angus wore a celeste blue superfine coat with mother-of-pearl buttons as big as crown pieces. The coat color enhanced the mischief in his vivid blue eyes. There was a subtle untamed look about him that added to his attractiveness as he sat his splendid horse. Angus could turn many a lady's head.

Seth was dressed more soberly in a dark-brown superfine, double-breasted coat with a high stand-fall collar and M-notch lapels. It sported slightly gathered shoulders with flapped pockets at the waist. The coat boasted fine gold buttons and fitted his broad shoulders to perfection. His hair was not cut quite as short as Angus' or as fashion dictated, for it curled slightly along his collar. He sat his horse with command. His black hair and high cheekbones added greatly to the air of mystery that surrounded him.

Both were amazed at the array of carriages and horsemen crowding the paths and the elegant members of the *ton*, who congregated to see and be seen. The way was constantly hampered by people stopping to talk or to take a walking acquaintance up into a vehicle.

"If you thought to ride, Angus, I fear you're to be disappointed. There's no room for a real gallop."

A short distance into the park they were hailed by Lord Charling. Mounted on a handsome gray gelding he was talking to two fashionably dressed ladies in an elegant barouche.

Lady Ansley did not much care for Lord Charling and would warn her niece about him as soon as he took his leave. She was a renowned beauty, the darling of Lord Ansley, and considered an arbiter of what was fashionable. She wielded almost as much power as the patronesses of Almack's, for if her door was open to one, every door was likewise open.

She rested back, listening to Lord Charling, amused by his inveigling ways. He was forever striving to be in everyone's good graces while he fleeced their sons or husbands. Her eyes traveled to the two approaching gentlemen. She was much taken by their appearance and intrigued by the dark-haired gentleman with the gray-green eyes. He had looked directly into her eyes upon his approach, and while his gaze was not bold, it was compelling.

"Lady Ansley, may I present two American friends, Mr. Seth Blakewell and Mr. Angus Grey?" Lord Charling asked.

She nodded regally and her ostrich feathers floated gently with the movement. "It is a pleasure. We hope you find your visit to our shores most interesting. May I make known to you my niece, Lady Markham?" Blakewell, she thought, how interesting.

Angus smiled and greeted them both, but his eyes strayed to the blushing girl who sat across from her aunt. A tiny young lady with brown curls peeking out of her yellow silk bonnet, she smiled and a pair of dimples appeared. She lowered her eyes and Angus lost his heart.

Lady Ansley watched this exchange and wondered if these men should be introduced to her niece. One cannot be too careful, she thought. There were no titles here—well, of course not, they're Americans. She wasn't quite sure which was worse.

She glanced up to find Seth's strange, smoky eyes lingering on her. The man was exceptionally captivating. There was an allusive quality about him, and she was immediately lifted from the boredom in which she had been languishing.

"I'm having a small gathering Thursday, Lord Charling.

Would you do me the honor of bringing Mr. Blakewell and Mr. Grey? If that is agreeable to you, gentlemen,'' she said softly in a pleasing, lyrical voice.

It was agreed then, with much enthusiasm by Lord Charling, that they would be most delighted to attend.

Lady Ansley motioned her driver to continue with a wave of her dainty lavender kid-gloved hand.

''Small gathering, not likely! It'll be a crush. You'll have entry into every house in London,'' Lord Charling exclaimed as soon as Lady Ansley was out of earshot. Claiming a triumph for his companions, he truly spoke for himself. He was gratified; it had been some time since he had received an invitation to one of her entertainments. Lord Charling glanced speculatively at Mr. Blakewell and wondered if he were the reason. He had noted Lady Ansley's interest in the handsome American. Since his mark was often in the latest gossip, he decided this possibility might prove both advantageous and amusing.

Lord Charling was correct in his estimate of the Lady Ansley's gatherings. Carriages lined the drive to the entrance, and it was several minutes before the expert coachman could even maneuver the vehicle near the portico. Finally they alighted from the carriage and entered the pilaster-framed door of the handsome Georgian house.

Seth and Angus, looking ruggedly handsome in evening dress, were greeted by Lord and Lady Ansley at the foot of the steps in the entrance hall. Lord Ansley was considerably older than his stylish wife, and he stood with beaming pride greeting his guests.

Lady Ansley, looking ravishing in a gown of silver threaded cream silk, graciously held out her hand in welcome. ''Edward, may I introduce you to the two Americans I told you about, Mr. Blakewell and Mr. Grey?''

"Welcome! We are pleased to have you join us this evening. You must tell us how things go in the colonies these days," Lord Ashley said.

Angus started to say that the colonies no longer existed, but discreetly held his words.

"You are kind to extend this invitation," Seth said as he bowed over Lady Ansley's hand.

She watched him rather closely. "Do make yourself at home and I shall later introduce you to many of our other guests."

The two gentlemen bowed and moved up the steps to the ballroom.

"Fancy, I'd say. Nothing like this in Savannah," Angus whispered, gazing about the magnificent hall and stairwell.

Seth laughed. "Hardly, but it will be an education, I'm sure."

"For what? Unless you're beginning to take this earl business seriously," Angus answered. He was becoming a little uncomfortable with the thronging guests.

Ladies dressed in elegant gowns and sparkling jewels moved with such assured grace that they seemed to Angus to be unapproachable. Music from a hidden orchestra offered a background to the hum of voices and lilting laughter as they entered the large gold-and-white ballroom. A thousand candles glittered in the crystal chandeliers that hung from beautifully carved paterae. The shimmering flames reflected in the gilded mirrors that lined the walls. This sparkling world was an impressive sight for the gentlemen from the edge of a frontier.

"Don't ogle, Seth. You look like a country flat," Angus teased.

Seth laughed, his eyes scanning the elegant ballroom. The smile faded and he frowned ever so slightly. Just why in hell was he even attending, he wondered. It seemed to him he was wide of the mark in what he had originally thought this visit would be . . .

Before the evening was over, Lady Ansley had introduced them to many of her illustrious guests. Both Seth and Angus danced many times.

Angus stood up once with Lady Markham. She looked lovely in her white gown tied high with blue ribbons. He blushed as much as the youthful lady, and had about as much experience on a dance floor as she. The opportunity was welcome, and he fervently hoped he had made a favorable impression on her.

Whether the evening was a success or not, Seth couldn't say, but Angus whistled a merry tune all the way home in the carriage.

It seems, thought Seth, my friend enjoyed himself more than he might care to admit.

6

Annemarie took to the idea of their journey with vigor. Somewhat surprised, Caroline was nevertheless satisfied with her daughter's ready acquiescence. She studied her daughter's face, noting her radiance and shining eyes. This mystified Caroline, but only momentarily. She simply attributed this change to Annemarie's understanding of the wisdom of her decision.

Annemarie was behaving in a manner that Caroline called "agreeable," and she expressed that fact to Mr. Marshall.

She even went so far as to compliment her daughter for her obvious cooperation in the need to find an appropriate suitor and husband.

Anne smiled to herself on these occasions, for she well understood her compliance: she hoped to meet Mr. Blakewell again.

Within the week, the household was thrown into turmoil with Caroline's preparations for the trip to London. Wardrobes were carefully checked to see what was suitable to take and if a bit of lace or a change of ribbon could improve a gown or bonnet.

Stepping over trunks crowding the upper hall, Quentin remarked, "I doubt if Queen Elizabeth spent more effort on her yearly progresses."

Caroline scoffed, seeing no humor in the remark.

"Quentin, you just do not see the importance in all this work I'm doing. Actually, with my careful scrutiny and subtle changes of our gowns, I'm saving you many pounds."

Marshall doubted the truth of her claim, but nodded as he made a swift retreat.

The servants sighed a prayer of thanksgiving when, at last, the family departed. The trip proved uneventful, but not silent. Caroline's whining complaints concerning the josting of the carriage on the rough roads accompanied the travelers.

Graciously welcomed into the comfortable home of Sir Devon Sutton on Green Street, Caroline basked in the consequence it gave her. Her complaints diminished to an occasional disapproving sniff.

Devon's wife, Sissy—as she was called instead of her given name of Sara—was a modest, agreeable matron whose greatest interest lay in the events that concerned her family. She was not a leader in the fashionable world but was accounted to be most pleasant and, therefore, well-liked.

The Sutton family consisted of one married son and two daughters who had made fortunate marriages. Sissy's life centered on her grandchildren, who, according to her testimony, were the brightest and best-mannered children to ever grace the earth.

Devon, a devoted family man, was far removed from the inner circle of cronies who surrounded the Prince of Wales. While never interested in the extravagant excesses of that rather notorious group, he much preferred town life. In fact, he hated country life, and for that reason Sutton Hall had been deeded to Caroline as her marriage settlement.

Quentin Marshall had little in common with his brother-in-law, but was glad for his connections. He was always alert to any advantage he might acquire to further his investment schemes.

Having settled in and rested a few days, Caroline, Sissy, and Anne set out to purchase the necessary frocks and accessories required in seeking a husband. During Anne's previous come-out, Caroline had dressed her in the fussy white dresses suited for the more diminutive ladies. The result had been a self-conscious young lady feeling very much like an overdressed giant.

"I am hoping for simpler lines in my gowns this Season," Anne announced when they entered Madame Claudine's shop.

"Annemarie, you must take our experienced advice: You're most apt to choose some far from appropriate gown," Caroline admonished.

"Anne is tall and stately, certainly no pocket Venus. Let us choose styles that enhance her regal bearing. We'll leave the ruffles and bows to the more diminutive miss," Sissy said with a smile that was impossible to refute.

Caroline viewed her daughter with a new appraisal and nodded reluctantly. The little pinched expression made it apparent she was skeptical.

Sissy, who had successfully launched two daughters, lent support to Anne's insistence on stylish gowns of simpler lines. Therefore, Sissy's and Anne's choices luckily prevailed. Dozens of smart gowns, habits, and walking dresses were ordered. Elated with their selections, Anne knew she would feel more confident if she did not resemble an overstuffed china doll.

Caroline eagerly threw herself into the project of her own dresses, which translated into a bevy of ostentatious designs. Her delight in frills knew no bounds, and she smugly considered her choices to be superior.

Next, the three ladies spent an afternoon purchasing bonnets, gloves, ribbons, and all that is deemed necessary

for a well-dressed lady of fashion. They returned home tired
and happy. Anne thankfully hugged Sissy for her kind
support. Sissy returned a smile of understanding.

Devon shared ardent equestrian interests with Quentin and
Annemarie. The love of horses and the hunt still fascinated
him. He made several trips each year to Sutton Hall merely
to ride to the hounds, and he kept a fine stable of horses in
London.

The first morning, following the delivery of a new riding
habit, Anne quickly dressed for a promised canter in the park.
Lord Sutton had previously offered a lovely spirited chestnut
named Rusty for Annemarie's use. Quentin happily agreed
to accompany her, rather than an appointed groom, stating
he was as eager as his daughter for a bit of exercise.

The stylish bronze velvet habit, trimmed with black braid
in a military fashion, which was all the rage, looked
absolutely smashing on Annemarie. A double row of black
frogs decorated the fitted jacket, which sported bold brass
buttons. A small black hat sat at a saucy angle, creating a
contrast to her golden-brown hair. Her sherry-flecked hazel
eyes glowed in response to the bronze habit.

"You look wonderful, Annemarie. Perhaps your mother
is correct. London may well suit you," Marshall teased as
he gave her a foot into the saddle.

"Your approval is flattering, but I'll tell you a secret: I'd
rather be at Sutton Hall on Taliesin's back riding the fields
unhampered by skirts," she teased.

"Hardly a secret, my dear."

Anne made herself comfortable in the sidesaddle, wishing,
all the while, she were astride Taliesin. London was no place
for that spirited animal, she knew. Still, she was content to
be on horseback and beamed with delight as they trotted
through the streets toward the park.

Since they entered Hyde Park at an early hour and few

riders were about, Anne turned and challenged her father. "I'll race you to the end of the path," she called over her shoulder.

"Done! If you'll not tell your mother . . . She would admonish me for allowing what she would term unseemly behavior." He set his horse into swift motion.

Annemarie felt the sense of freedom found only on the back of a galloping horse. Exhilaration sped through her body as the cool air rushed past her cheeks, and her spirits soared.

Laughing together, they finished the sprint to the end of the path and were reigning in for a more sedate return when Seth Blakewell, accompanied by his friend Mr. Grey, happened along.

"Good morning, Squire Marshall and Miss Marshall," Seth greeted them with undisguised pleasure.

Anne returned the greeting with a nod and a skip of her heart; he was more attractive than she had remembered. Hating the flush that rose in her cheeks, she frowned slightly at her telltale reaction.

Seth took in every detail of this handsome woman and felt a slight pang, for he thought the frown directed at him. "I hope we are not impeding your ride," he apologized.

"Nonsense, we're about to make our return ride. Do join us," Quentin said.

The path was narrow and Squire Marshall was anxious to speak with Seth, so that left Mr. Grey to ride beside Miss Marshall.

Sitting tall and easy in his saddle, Seth masked the disdain in which he held Quentin Marshall. He listened with feigned courtesy and answered the vague questions Squire Marshall put to him.

The Squire was somewhat suspicious and apprehensive of Mr. Blakewell, wondering who he was. Had John lived and was this his son returned to claim his rights? he wondered.

He could not ask directly, but remembering Cecil's warning, he felt compelled to seek some answers.

"How do you find our country? I daresay a vast difference from the United States," Marshall asked.

Seth sent him a questioning look. "Indeed, vastly different. As I mentioned during luncheon at Sutton Hall, my plantation is on the edge of the frontier, quite uncivilized by your standards. Still, opportunity abounds for anyone willing to work. I have built up a very profitable shipping trade out of Savannah. The politics of our countries have allowed that possibility, if one is prepared to take the risks. English buyers are eager to receive my tobacco and cotton." Seth was becoming a little tired of touting his business, but realized it was necessary to influence Marshall.

"Doesn't that make you an outlaw, or at least less than patriotic to your country?" Quentin asked with increased interest. Here perhaps was a man who looked at life as he did: one who was not above bending the law for a profit.

Seth read the thought in his eyes and smiled. His gaze rested on the squire's face as he regarded Quentin a moment. "I prefer the word *privateer*. We are a nation of individuals. Our allegiance is surpassed by none, but I am a Georgian first and foremost. Not all the government's decrees suit us. We choose to ignore those we don't agree with, but make no mistake we are united and loyal."

"Oh, I meant no offense. It's just that I'm a man of commerce myself and find myself intrigued by your endeavors," Marshall added hastily.

A derisive smile played on Seth's mouth. His eyes traveled to the back of Miss Marshall, who was in conversation with Angus. He turned his head sharply to the gentleman riding next to him, a thoughtful look upon his face.

"Opportunities are great for a daring man here in England. I've been noting the docking problems along the Thames.

There is money to be made. I'm considering some options myself,'' Seth said, his eyes glittering a moment as he set his snare.

Quentin's interest was instantly peaked. He relaxed his guard, deciding Seth was not related to John Blakewell, or if he was, then he did not know anything of the shooting, impressment, and . . . He did not finish the reflection. Marshall was sure Blakewell would not be discussing business with a man he suspected of a possible crime against John Blakewell.

Surprisingly, he disregarded the ring worn by the American. The reason for this stemmed from his interest in the opportunities mentioned. Therefore, Marshall foolishly dismissed his suspicion with a great sigh, assuming the name was a mere coincidence. Surely, if Blakewell was related to John, he would make it known.

Dismissing his concern by allowing it probably came from Cecil's foolish fears, which stemmed from his guilty conscience. He would inform Cecil that the names were mere coincidence as soon as possible.

"What sort of options?" Quentin asked, his eagerness all too obvious.

"Are you familiar with the ingenious plan for shortening the journey up the Thames proposed in 1796?" Seth smoothly asked.

Marshall vaguely remembered such a plan and shook his head in confirmation.

Seth smiled slightly. Good, he thought. "Wiley Reveley, a rather brilliant architect and engineer, suggested cutting a channel three-quarters of a mile long to join up Blakewell and Limehouse reaches. It would save hours or even days on the length of the journey, depending on the winds."

"Indeed? Whatever happened to the proposal?" Quentin asked.

"I shall show you the drawings. The cut channel would become the main course of the river and would leave the great horseshoe and the two other loops for conversion into docks. I've seen the West India Docks, but far more are needed."

"Why wasn't the plan executed? No money?" Marshall asked.

"No, declared too difficult to accomplish, but I doubt that," Seth lied.

"It cost four million pounds for the new City docks at Wapping. So I assume you're speaking of a fortune needed in capital for the land as well as the labor and engineering," Quentin pressed.

"Certainly, but the rewards would soon pay off the expenditures. The plan would have to be modified now, of course. It's only an idea I'm toying with. May have no merit, but I intend to pursue the study of it."

"Do keep me informed. I am a man of business and keen on new ideas," Squire Marshall said.

Seth turned and nodded. His green-gray eyes and disarming smile sent a little shiver down Marshall's spine. I know nothing about him, Quentin thought. Once more he foolishly dismissed his feeling of unease; Squire Marshall had an overrated opinion of his ability to judge people.

Anne was being charmed by personable Angus. His open and easy manner was so very different from any other young men she had previously met. There were no studied compliments and he spoke to her as an equal. This both surprised and delighted her.

"Do you also have a plantation?" she asked.

"No, my family does. I'm a lawyer, but I'd rather be out in the wilderness hunting and trapping. Do so, as often as I can. Seth joins me. We roam the land and sleep under the stars. The freedom and beauty of the land are beyond description, and totally intoxicating. We're always reluctant to return, but duty seems to call us more often the older we get. Ah, the joys of a carefree young man," he said.

Anne watched him with interest. He held none of the serious demeanor of English barristers.

Seth found himself bored, wishing he could maneuver his horse next to the young lady. What in the devil was Angus telling her? he wondered. He could hear her soft laughter and was becoming annoyed with Squire Marshall's unending recounting of his various achievements. He soon was not even pretending to listen; he watched Miss Marshall.

Anne was sure she could feel Mr. Blakewell's eyes on her, and she resisted the impulse to turn and peep. Where the path widened at the entrance of the park, Mr. Blakewell maneuvered his horse to her side.

"Miss Marshall, I regret not having the chance to ride next to you. But it is a pleasure to see you again," he said.

"Yes, I am pleased we meet again. Mr. Grey has been telling such fascinating tales of your homeland," she said, and looked to him. Their eyes held a moment.

"Do you ride often while in London?" he asked.

"Yes, with every excuse I can make," she replied. She laughed, sending a dancing sparkle to her hazel eyes. "Although it is impossible to experience a really strenuous ride. You'll find riding in London a social event, not intended for exercise. That is why we ride early in the morning."

"Perhaps you would do the honor of riding out with me one morning."

Anne glanced to her father.

"That would be most agreeable, Mr. Blakewell. You have my permission," Marshall interjected, knowing it would facilitate the continuance of the acquaintance.

Seth quickly seized this opportunity. "Perhaps, if the weather holds, you might ride with me tomorrow morning."

Anne's horse shied a little, and she steadied it. His large stallion was making her horse as nervous as its owner was making her. The idea struck her as amusing. She again raised her eyes to Seth's and was surprised by the directness of his gaze.

She quickly lowered hers and said, "Thank you, I should enjoy a ride tomorrow." Great heavens, I'm acting akin to a silly schoolgirl, she reasoned with chagrin.

When at last they parted, Anne was fascinated by the tall, dark-haired gentleman. She would eagerly await the following morning.

The return ride with her father was quiet, for neither spoke. Both were involved in their own thoughts, which centered on the handsome American for different reasons.

Arriving back at the Sutton home, Anne went directly to her room to change. An expression of consternation played on her even features. Her qualm concerned her mother's reaction to their meeting with Mr. Blakewell and her intended ride. A groom would be in attendance, to be sure, but Anne understood her mother would not consider Mr. Blakewell an acceptable suitor. Anne shrugged. If that was what he was . . . But surely he must be interested, she mused, merely by the expression in his eyes. The remembered impact of his gaze sent a shiver down her spine.

Anne was correct in her assessment of her mother's response. Caroline was incensed.

"We know nothing of this foreigner. Quentin, how could you? He is not of the *ton*. Simply not acceptable. Have you lost your reason? I will not tolerate this. She must make a suitable alliance now," Caroline chided when they were alone in their bedchamber.

Quentin Marshall was taken aback by the intensity of his wife's objections. He could hardly confess to her that he was in hopes of a commercial agreement with the American nabob.

"My dear, you make too much of it," he exclaimed. Then to placate her he added, "I've spoken with Lord Blakewell and we have agreed that a marriage between Anthony and Annemarie would be an excellent arrangement. Anthony is to begin his suit while we are in London," Quentin explained.

Caroline's eyes widened. "How marvelous! The future heir to the Earl of Chathram!"

Marshall nodded. He hoped Annemarie would agree.

"It is fortunate they grew up together, because I speak truthfully, she could hope for no more. Good heavens, such good news! Why didn't you tell me sooner?" she asked.

"Thought it would be best to let it seem a natural event. Don't make too much of it or Annemarie will balk," he warned.

"She will not! She will do as she is told. How famous! I couldn't be more pleased. I think you should advise her of this fortunate news," Caroline said.

"All in good time. I will talk with Lord Anthony as soon as possible," Quentin replied.

"I cannot approve her riding out with this Mr. Blakewell. Do you think it odd that this American has the same last name?" Caroline asked.

"Hardly, my dear, since most of the colonies were settled by Englishmen. I'm sure there are also Suttons and Marshalls living there."

7

The autumn storm broke before dawn, pelting the window with a hard, driving rain. Annemarie awoke to the relentless sound of rolling thunder and the pinging of water against the window. She snuggled down among the warm coverlets tucked up to her chin, listening with a pang of disappointment. If her guess was correct, it was a storm that would settle in for the day.

There would be no canter in the park this morning. A frown wrinkled her smooth brow at the thought. Realizing the depth of her disappointment, she allowed a spirited word to escape her lips. Mr. Blakewell was an intriguing man, and she longed to have the opportunity to ride with him.

Ensconced in eiderdown, she thought of his rugged, handsome face, but knew it was the intensity of his eyes, when they lingered on her, that sent her pulse racing. There would be another opportunity, she decided, trying to cheer herself, and prayed that would be so.

When Anne reached the breakfast room later in the morning, the rain continued sending streams of water down the mullioned windowpanes. It was as gray and bleak a day as could be expected this time of year. Anne watched the window a moment before she took her place at the table.

Greeting her mother and Aunt Sissy, Anne took in the appearance of both ladies and was touched by the pleasant serenity of her aunt. Somehow her mother never managed to seem genuinely happy—smugly proud on occasion, but never did she emanate Sissy's contentment. How sad, Anne thought, for the idea hit her with some force. What makes two people view life so differently?

Caroline smiled. "Well, there will be no outing with the American today," she said, her pleasure at the prospect unmasked.

Annemarie looked at her mother and shrugged. "Perhaps another time."

"Well, I can't say I approve. We know nothing of him. I am very hopeful you do not make it known he is a serious suitor," Caroline said, buttering a roll.

"Mother, a ride in the park does not constitute a serious intention of matrimony. You make far too much of a mere outing," Anne said.

Caroline arched an eyebrow. "One simply cannot be too careful, my dear. Your father has spoken with Lord Cecil Blakewell, and he is most desirous that Lord Anthony pay you court. I expect you to receive him with graciousness."

Anne raised her head in surprise. "I should always receive Anthony with graciousness. He is a dear friend. I have never thought of him in the light of a suitor," she said with creeping apprehension.

"Well, do so. He is most suitable. A perfect match," her mother ordered in a voice that brooked no argument.

Anne had no intention of arguing. She would learn just what feelings Lord Anthony held, if any. They had known each other all their lives. Actually, they were more like brother and sister in their easy camaraderie. She sincerely doubted whether Anthony held any emotion for her other than great friendship.

"From all that I hear, Lord Anthony enjoys the rather dubious diversions of London. I am told he often frequents the gaming hells. It is general knowledge he has lost vast sums of late. I should think twice before I align myself with a gambler, friend or no,'' Anne sharply replied.

"You must not take gossip as gospel, Annemarie. Sometimes all that is needed for a young man to settle down is a good and sensible wife. And that you most undoubtedly would be,'' Caroline said, and it sounded more like an accusation than a virtue.

A small smile lifted the corners of Anne's full mouth. She would refrain from comment, but she would wed only when her heart was engaged.

Aunt Sissy sat in embarrassed silence. Coming to the aid of her much-loved niece, she said, "Caroline, a ride in the park with a handsome gentleman could only raise a young lady's worth as a captivating charmer. It never hurts to have a dozen swarming swains."

Caroline scoffed. Happily, the conversation turned to different topics, and Anne escaped to her bedroom at the first opportunity.

A lovely bouquet and a note were delivered by one of Mr. Seth Blakewell's footmen. Opening the crisp seal, Annemarie read the letter of apology written in a strong hand.

My dear Miss Marshall,
    Since the weather lies beyond my power to command, I regret, sincerely, the postponement of our outing. I look forward to riding with you and hope to claim that pleasure the first sunny day.

Disappointed, she folded the letter and carefully tucked it away. Catching her reflection in the mirror, she ran her hands along her face, turning this way and that. All she saw was a tall young woman of passable looks, hardly a belle of the first order.

A restlessness grew from her disappointment and she aimlessly wandered about her room. London society was a bore, and London during inclement weather was positively oppressing. At least in the country there was much to do; she would have spent such a morning with her horses. Anne decided that the possibility of seeing Mr. Blakewell was the sole reason making this visit bearable. Perhaps that is a mistake, she mused. She stopped, took one last survey at her reflection, and softly laughed. My, what unaccountable avenues one's mind will travel all because of a particularly attractive man, she thought.

The rain continued, clearing finally in the afternoon of the third day. They were to attend a small gathering given by Lord and Lady Rothier, close friends of Sissy and Devon. Sissy had spoken to Lady Rothier, who immediately issued an invitation to Seth Blakewell and Angus Grey. This bit of information was not imparted to her guests.

The weather had left Anne so restless that she was genuinely pleased to be attending a party. She wore a silk gown of pale, apple green, simply cut, high under the bosom and dropping in soft pleats. It displayed her creamy shoulders and shapely figure with elegant simplicity. Her hair was arranged on top of her head with tendrils curling down the sides of her face. The style added to her height but drew attention to her almond-shaped eyes and displayed her long neck to advantage.

Annemarie was pleased with her appearance. A small knot tightened in her stomach as she hoped against hope Seth Blakewell would be attending the evening's event. She thought that highly unlikely, and resigned herself to the hope of riding with him in the near future.

When Anne descended the steps to her waiting family, Caroline was astonished at how lovely her daughter looked.

"My dear, that gown is exceptionally suited to you," she

said, noticing the stately elegance of her daughter for the first time.

Mr. Marshall beamed with pride. She's a fine-looking girl, he thought.

Sissy hugged her niece. "You're lovely, Annemarie."

Anne was pleased with such attention, for she had in no way thought of herself in that light, and while she knew she looked her best, she understood her audience was decidedly partial.

Confidence was Anne's companion upon entering the Rothier ballroom a short while later. She paused at the entrance, arrested by the splendor of the decor. Asters and mums banked the walls, transforming it into an autumn garden. Warmth and laughter pervaded the room as the orchestra played a merry country set for the pleasure of the dancing guests. A soft smile turned the corners of her mouth, and a delighted sparkle glimmered in her eyes at the enchanting scene.

Lady Rothier took Annemarie in hand and proceeded to introduce her to the most interesting guests. She was pleased to have the opportunity to assist her friend's striking niece. Anne's newfound assurance allowed her to move with regal grace, thereby receiving many admiring glances and myriad compliments. This translated in a sparkling response, for she was enjoying herself beyond her previous imagination and wondered why all this had so overwhelmed her only a few years ago.

Her back was toward the entrance, so she missed the arrival of the American gentleman who had too often been on her mind. Sissy opened her fan to cover the smile that appeared on her lips at the gasp escaping Caroline Marshall's mouth.

Caroline turned to her sister-in-law. "Whatever is he here for?" she whispered testily.

Sissy turned wide, innocent eyes to her. "Why to enjoy the entertainment, I presume."

Caroline issued a very unattractive snort.

Seth quickly scanned the ballroom. He espied Miss Marshall immediately, turned, and gave Angus a wink. In the direct manner of his countrymen, he purposefully walked toward the tall, elegant figure from which his eyes never wavered. Angus trailed behind feeling a little like a baby duck in its mother's wake. He chuckled at the idea.

"Ah, Mr. Blakewell, Mr. Grey, so kind of you to come," Lady Rothier said as she extended her hand in turn to each gentleman. I understand Sissy's intervention; they are attractive, she mused. No wonder Sissy is playing Cupid.

Anne twirled around, her eyes wide with surprise.

"Good evening, Lady Rothier. Thank you for your kind invitation," Seth said, bowing over her hand.

"Are you acquainted with Miss Marshall?" she asked as she had been instructed by her dear friend.

"Yes. Good evening, Miss Marshall. It is a pleasure to see you again," he said.

Anne looked at the rich black hair of his head as he bowed. Her faculties seemed to go blank. He lifted his eyes to hers as he straightened. The smoky gray-green flickered with a glint of fire. Her lips trembled slightly as she attempted to put on a society smile. She beheld his high cheekbones and sensuous mouth. He is impressive, she thought, and searched for something to say.

"I hope you are enjoying London, Mr. Blakewell," she said, thinking the comment inane. If not inane, then definitely dull. The man had the power to leave her witless.

"The weather has robbed me of what I desired most to do," he said, extending his hand. "Do favor me with this dance and rectify what the weather denied me."

Anne glanced at Lady Rothier, who was taking in his

cryptic remark with interest. "Yes, do enjoy yourselves," Lady Rothier said. "I must continue to greet my guests. Mr. Grey, do accompany me, there are several people I want you to meet." Angus happily agreed; he had stood feeling somewhat *de trop*.

Anne placed her hand on Mr. Blakewell's arm as they moved to the dance floor to take their places in the set for the quadrille, the latest rage in London.

"You are even more enchanting than ever, Miss Marshall," he said, placing her hand on his arm to form the set. He looked into her tawny eyes and felt the power of her open gaze. His senses reeled. She is magnificent, he thought. A woman to stand beside a man. No fluttering, simpering girl, but a woman who could be a partner. An image of her with her hair down, tumbling over his pillows, flashed in his mind. He stored that thought to savor later.

"Perhaps the weather will now favor us. I expect to claim the ride you have so graciously promised me," he said.

"I shall anticipate it with great pleasure. In fact, I was disappointed when the rains prevented our outing."

The dance steps parted them as they glided through the pattern.

He smiled. No young lady he had met thus far would speak so honestly. When he took her hand once again, he tightened his hold ever so slightly.

Anne's pulses raced. Here was a man one could respect, not some mincing fob with silly, inane prattle.

"Are you enjoying your visit to England?" she asked, realizing she had already asked the question. Inane prattle, she thought, just listen to me!

"At this moment, I am," he said, looking down into her eyes.

Anne blushed and hated herself for so obvious a reaction. "Will you be staying long?"

"As long as it takes to finish what I came to accomplish."

"And what is that?"

"I'm no longer sure," he whispered as they were parted again by the pattern of the dance steps.

Anne glanced over her shoulder as she advanced to her next partner. Seth's eyes followed her movements.

The music ended and Seth extended his arm to her. They walked together in silence. This moment was too important. Their awareness of each other bound them together in their own thoughts.

Anne was amazed that she felt almost bereft when they returned to her mother.

"Thank you, Miss Marshall. May I claim another dance later?"

"Yes, I would be honored," she answered. He held her gaze a moment and bowed to take his leave.

"Well, he is much too direct," Caroline scoffed.

"Yes, isn't he?" Anne smiled slightly.

"A handsome man, to be sure," Sissy added.

Caroline frowned. "Lacks polish and breeding. One can always tell."

Seth did not dance again. He stood back against the wall with his arms folded and watched the dancers. His keen eyes remained on Annemarie as she swirled with grace in the arms of her other partners. He knew, having held her in his arms, he could never be the same again.

"Are you going to stand here all evening? You look like a permanent fixture on the wall," Angus asked, coming up to his comrade.

Seth was startled by the interruption of his reverie. "I, er, was just thinking," Seth weakly explained.

"It is unmistakable just what you are thinking," Angus replied. "You ought not be so obvious."

"What in the devil do you mean?" Seth said, standing away from the wall and dropping his arms.

"Why, the Marshall chit. She has your eye," Angus continued in a teasing way. "And a fine example of womanhood, I'll agree."

"You're impertinent. You know not of what you speak," Seth said.

"You're correct on one count only, but then, I've always been impertinent."

"I don't think you have much to talk about. Doesn't the Lady Markham have you making calf eyes?"

"Yes, that is why I can recognize a man trapped in a feminine web," Angus said.

"Hardly trapped, Angus. You must admit, she's magnificent."

"Best beware, unless you count on remaining as a dandified earl," Angus said.

"Enough of this conversation. Let us get some refreshment," Seth said, beginning to move to the door of the ballroom.

Anne watched him leave. She had kept him in her eyes as she executed the various dances. Her flushed cheeks and sparkling eyes added to her charm. She was asked to partner every dance.

A satisfied expression settled on Caroline's face. Anne was a decided success.

The night was half-gone when Lord Anthony Blakewell arrived with several young blades, and Caroline quickly caught his attention. Lord Anthony languidly made his way toward her. He was tall and rather thin. His recent life showed on his youthful face, with slight rings under his eyes and a pallor to his skin.

"Good evening, Mrs. Marshall. I'm told that Annemarie is with you," he said searching the room with his eyes.

"Yes, we've come for the little Season. She's quite a success," Caroline added.

"She's always been a success," he replied as he saw his childhood friend being escorted from the dance floor. She looks outstanding, he thought as he surveyed her simply cut gown.

"Anthony, how famous to see you," Anne said, extending her hand.

"Likewise, dear friend. It is grand to find you looking so charming. I daresay you've been besieged. Is there the possibility of my claiming a dance? Perhaps the dinner dance, and you can tell me all about the spectacular new Irish hunter you now own. I vow he's won your heart."

"Yes, he is magnificent. You will see Taliesin when we go down for the hunt party and ball," Anne answered with animated enthusiasm.

Anthony laughed. "You've not changed one iota. You may look suited to the dance floor, but it is the back of a horse that makes your eyes shine."

Anne tilted her head a bit. "You understand me far too well. I thought I should go mad with these last days of rain. Why are you be so fond London with its confining rain?"

Lord Anthony frowned slightly. "It has its diversions. You know the country bores me. A hunt now and again is about all I care to have. Come, fair friend, dance with me if you're not promised."

Annemarie took his extended arm just as Seth and Angus reentered the ballroom. Seth looked for Anne and saw her walking to the dance floor with a young man. She was smiling and laughing with her partner, and Seth thought she was far more interested in him than she had been with her previous partners. There was something about this man. Seth frowned.

Just then Squire Marshall greeted him. "Good evening, Mr. Blakewell. Have you been pursuing your dock interest?" he blatantly asked.

Seth's eyes narrowed. The man never seemed to improve. It was not hard to imagine him in the plot against his father. Seth's eyes traveled to Annemarie. He did not answer Squire Marshall's question. His interest in Miss Marshall was complicating his plans, and his resolve faltered with doubts. How could he bring down a man who was the father of a lady he wished to pursue? Marshall's voice interrupted his thoughts.

"That is Lord Anthony Blakewell dancing with my daughter. Have you met him?" Marshall asked.

Seth stiffened, his jaw muscles tightened. His eyes traveled to those of Angus. Angus raised an eyebrow and glanced over to the dancing couple.

"No, I have not had the honor. Is he Cecil's son?" Seth asked.

"Yes. Are you acquainted with Cecil Blakewell?" Quentin asked anxiously.

"Not yet," Seth said, "but I intend to be. Will you introduce us?"

"Happy to. Should be interested in the fact your last names are the same. American and all, you understand. Don't suppose you're somehow related. What an interesting idea," Squire Marshall said, feeling the ominous twinge again. Suppose John had survived, he thought, and a chill ran down through his body. No, not likely. Blakewell would have inquired of him. Mere coincidence, once again, Marshall reassured himself.

"Annemarie and Anthony are to be betrothed this Season. They've known each other for years, and it will be an excellent match." There was a boastful pride in his utterance.

Seth's head snapped around; his eyes leveled fury on

Squire Marshall. The pompous ass! Quickly recovering, Seth replied, "I'm meeting with some financial backers on the dock project. I'll call on you in a day or so to see if you're still interested." Turning swiftly on his heel, Seth left the company of Squire Marshall and the assembled guests. There remained no lingering doubts in Seth Blakewell's mind. He knew just where he was headed.

8

Immediately upon leaving Lord and Lady Rothier's ball, Seth realized how foolish his jealous reaction had been. To turn heel and run like a scared rabbit . . . How easily he had been routed! Lord, if he wanted to win the battle for the lady's hand, he shouldn't have quit the field, he admonished himself a dozen times.

"Seth, stop chastising yourself. You've got time to make your suit. You can't know for sure if she'll become engaged to Anthony. I've never known you so cast down. When have you ever failed at something you truly wanted?" Angus asked, lengthening his step to keep up with Seth.

They hurried along St. James Street to join Lord Charling at White's Club as Seth translated his frustration into long swift strides. "This time I'm not so confident. Let's forget it for now and spend the remaining evening fleecing Charling."

Angus sent his friend a concerned look and nodded in agreement.

Later that evening, they sat in White's enjoying a late brandy and discussing the famous betting book when Theodore Hook happened by.

"Hook," Charling said, hailing the notorious gentlemen. "Allow me to make two American visitors known to you."

Theodore Hook, a dandy with long sideburns and exaggerated high point collars—so high, in fact, he could barely turn his head—approached them with a smile and genial manner.

"Good evening, gentlemen," he said.

"May I present Mr. Blakewell and Mr. Grey of Georgia?"

The men shook hands and Charling resumed his discussion of the betting book. "I was telling them of the three-thousand-pound bet made by Lord Arlington on which of two raindrops would reach the bottom of a windowpane first."

Hook chuckled.

"Ah, but you're the one to have accomplished the coup de grace of all time," Charling said with more than a little awe and respect.

"It was no such thing. An easy matter to be sure," Hook replied in false modesty.

"Nothing? Gentlemen, Mr. Hook achieved a bet of masterly proportions. Beau Brummell and Count d'Orsay may set fashion with their dazzling, exquisite cut of coat, and Sydney Smith and Henry Luttell win salience by their sharp wit, but Hook has won immortality by a bet," Charling claimed with a flourish of his hand.

"Immortality is doing it up a bit brown, don't you think? I merely relied on the word of a gentleman to carry if off," Hook replied, but his pleasure in the retelling brought a decided pride, which was interesting in a man who liked to deflate pomposity.

"Let us hear it from you. We'll get the facts," Lord Charling said, indicating a seat for Hook and ordering the gentleman a brandy.

Theodore Hook gleefully began the recitation he had made on many occasions. "I was with Sam Beazeley sauntering along Berners Street, which boasts, as you know, only modest rows of houses. I wagered I'd lay him a guinea in a week that any one of these nice, quiet dwellings would be the most famous in London. I pointed my cane at random to the Number Fifty-four house."

"How did you ever manage it?" Charling asked eager to hear the details.

"During the next few days I wrote several hundred letters to tradesmen all over London requesting goods to be delivered to Number Fifty-four at a certain time and date. Mrs. Tottingham happens to live there; she is a well-to-do widow, and that fact fell quite fortunately and unexpectedly into the plan. She is well-known among the tradesmen. Greengrocers, dairymen, bakers, coal merchants, and even an undertaker were summoned. A finishing touch don't you think?" He chuckled. "I had various goods such as china, books, glass, and even a harpsichord delivered. Beer was ordered by the dray and wine by the dozens of bottles."

Angus' eyes grew wide with delight. "All at the same time?" he asked.

"Yes, but it was the members of Parliament, lawyers, and preachers I invited on clever excuses, if I may be so immodest to say so, that made it so successful. I managed to lure the lord mayor, and the governor of the Bank of England, he on the pretext that an exposé of fraud by a clerk would be forthcoming. The Duke of Gloucester was actually enticed by the promise of a former royal servant, who had a deathbed confession to make to him."

"What genius! You should be in politics," Charling laughed.

"Certainly, the response was beyond anything I had envisioned. The confusion was enormous, with so many carts, carriages, and drays. Casks smashed and wine ran along the street with broken bottles. Horses fell, coach panels were smashed, and vegetables rolled into the gutters. Pickpockets had a very profitable day. I, of course, watched the whole melee behind a lace curtain from a window in a house directly across the street." He sighed with end of the tale. "It has, I fear, been embellished in the retelling many times over. But most important, I won my guinea."

Seth sat in amazement at the recitation of this frivolous, destructive event. "You mean everyone fell so easily in with the practical joke?"

"Indeed, we take our bets very seriously," Hook replied.

"It surpasses any bet I'm aware of in White's famous book," Charling said.

Hook nodded, but it was obvious he held the gullibility in disdain and was delighted with his practical joke, for it exposed the ridiculous high spirits that passed for amusement among the aristocrats. It did not occur to him that his act was irresponsible. He basked in his success.

"It has been a pleasure to meet you. I don't suppose you have such diverting events occurring in the colonies." He rose to take his leave.

"There doesn't seem to be the time. We are too busy working . . . I suppose. Never met anyone would think to do it. We are totally caught up in what needs to be done," Seth said.

"How exceedingly unfortunate," Hook said as he departed.

"What a tale. Is it true?" Angus asked.

"It is, and we heard of nothing else for weeks. The satirical cartoonists made much of the foolishness. There were some very red faces, I assure you," Charling said.

Seth was interested for other reasons. He thought he could use that very audacity and response to his advantage. The tale had taken his mind off the infuriating news he had received from Squire Marshall. He had been delayed by the attraction to Miss Marshall from the original intent of his visit to England. Now he was more determined than ever to make his presence known on behalf of his dead father's memory. He would use such gullibility to his advantage.

Annemarie restlessly waited, hoping Mr. Blakewell would pay a call. The weather was beautiful, perfect for riding. The leaves were blazing with autumn colors; the promising thought of sitting in a saddle next to the intriguing American haunted her thoughts. However, no word came from the elusive gentleman. She was perplexed, because she was sure he had been interested in furthering their acquaintance.

Three days passed and still no invitation was forthcoming. Perhaps, she thought, the direct manner and interest were just American traits and meant no more than the effusive compliments heard at any soiree. The thought sent her sagging spirits even lower.

Anthony, however, did call. He arranged to escort Anne for a ride in Green Park. As he waited in the salon for her, he paced the room, thinking about his wretched situation. He frowned, remembering the day his father had come up to London and placed the inevitable prospect of his betrothal to Annemarie. He had been summoned to the library, where his father awaited him.

"Be seated, Tony. I wish to speak to you about an essential matter," Lord Blakewell ordered, uncomfortable with the topic he was about to broach.

Cecil was tall and had the fair complexion, blue eyes, and light-brown hair that were characteristic of the Blakewells. His eyes held an evasive quality and he always carried the air of an injured man. It was oppressive to be in his company for long, without wondering what was amiss and if oneself was at fault. And so had his long-suffering wife felt before death parted their company.

Cecil cleared his throat. "It is time you married. I abhor the many tales that filter back to me. Your wastrel activities and pursuit of gambling are becoming scandalous. I no longer will tolerate them.''

Lord Blakewell held a silent, crusading hate for games of chance that stemmed from the fateful night that had ended with a shooting. He had never touched cards again.

Anthony shifted in his seat. He felt a flush spread over his face and perspiration bead on his forehead. Does my father know the extent of my debts? he wondered. He had continued in losing during these many weeks.

''I have drawn up a marriage contract with Squire Marshall, and it is our wish that you make a match with Annemarie. I know she brings only a modest dowry, but I think she would be a steadying influence on you.''

Sensing his father was less than happy over the proposed alliance, for he had mentioned her lack of a sizable dowry, Anthony could not understand his approval.

''I had not thought to marry yet. I'm young and could probably make a more profitable union.''

''Your reputation is suffering. You've not been notably circumspect. I hear the tales of your losses. How much are you in debt?''

Almost choking on his words, Anthony could barely utter them. ''Nothing to be concerned about. I've had a streak of luck, of late,'' he lied. For some strange reason he was not being pressed for payment, and the unexpected reprieve for payment had gone unexamined by him in the hopes he would have the money by the time the debts were called in. He carried the implausible optimism of the seasoned gambler for the next chance to win, and win big.

Lord Blakewell looked with disapproval at his son. He studied this tall, thin, young man dressed in the usual blue well-fitted coat and buff pantaloons. His handsome, thin face showed signs of dissipation at his young age. This is the scion of my family, Cecil thought derisively. ''You will begin to pay your court to Annemarie immediately. We'll plan on a spring wedding.''

"I'm sure Squire Marshall and especially Mrs. Marshall are beside themselves with joy at the fortunate choice for their daughter,'' Anthony added, sarcasm coloring his voice.

Fury rose in Lord Blakewell. "She's a fine lady. You may become a man under the responsibilities of a wife.''

"I like Annemarie well enough. She's been my friend for years. I do find her agreeable in all ways. It just surprises me that it is apparently a match you want. I don't understand it. The Marshalls are far below our social standing. They are accepted only through Mrs. Marshall's brother's influence.''

"That is not the point. Marry—and marry Annemarie Marshall—you will. I shall cut you off without a hint of regret if you defy me,'' Lord Blakewell bellowed. He detested this position forced upon him. Never would he have insisted on this match if not for the debt of honor owed Qeuntin for his help so long ago. It rankled his sense of proper position held by the Earls of Chathram. They did not marry daughters of country squires . . . But he had no choice.

Besides, he was nervous about the American lately come to London. Mr. Blakewell's inquiry and expressed desire to meet his father denoted an idea too horrible to contemplate. It would be best if Anthony was betrothed to Annemarie. The Earl of Chathram had always fairly doted on the child. His approval would now be of the utmost importance if the American began to play the devil.

Every argument Lord Anthony presented to his father was promptly dismissed. He was simply not given a choice, and he was puzzled at his father's insistence. It was definitely not a brilliant match for the future Earl of Chathram. Yet he had threatened to cut him off and the considerable debts— unknown to his father—hung over his head. He would receive a goodly portion from his mother's estate upon his marriage, and this means to pay the vowels tipped the scale.

Finally, Anthony agreed. "I shall do as you ask. Annemarie is acceptable. I'm fond of her." He knew she would spend her time in the country, giving him the freedom he sought to experience London life. He smiled. It might not be so bad, after all.

Lord Anthony bowed to his father's wish and began to pay court to Annemarie. Anthony stood in the Sutton salon waiting for Anne. His earlier interview with the squire now filled his mind. He frowned: the man was presumptuous.

Quentin Marshall, unaware Caroline had already mentioned the marriage possibility to his daughter, suggested to Lord Anthony that they not inform Anne about the intended betrothal. "It would be best," he suggested, "if you two young people become used to the idea of being together before we press Anne."

Lord Anthony, affronted by the implication, scowled.

Quentin, realizing the enormity of this tactless remark, hastily explained, "If we announce it too soon, Mrs. Marshall will become unbearable with plans. It will be best for us all if we just let matters take their natural course."

Nodding agreement, young Lord Blakewell saw the wisdom in this. The explanation did not seem like an affront to his desirability for Annemarie. Besides, he thought, it would give him a little time, and any number of things could happen before then.

Anthony's contemplation of his past interviews leading to his predicament was abruptly interrupted when Anne entered the room. He looked up to see her cross the room smiling, looking every inch a town beauty. They greeted each other with amity.

"We've a lovely day to ride," Anthony said, taking her arm to escort her to the waiting horses. Despite the circumstances, Anthony was pleased to be accompanying Anne on a ride in Green Park. Regardless of her family, he was truly fond of Anne. Beaming as he assisted her into the saddle of her horse, he gave her hand a slight squeeze.

"Thank you, Tony. I've looked forward to this outing. Riding is the one thing I miss dreadfully and there's little enough chance to do so in London," she said, happily arranging the skirt of her bronze velvet habit.

"You're looking grand, Anne. You may miss Surrey, but London obviously must agree with you. I've never seen you so stylish and beautiful," he said with the proud sincerity that came from his brotherly feelings toward her.

Anne turned to look at him. "I am not beautiful. Stylish, perhaps, but then Madame Claudine has a way of enhancing any woman." A golden twinkle danced in her eyes; the compliment was welcomed, for she valued his opinion.

"You've never believed in your attractiveness. Even when we were young, you made a point of your feelings. It seems your beauty is one that blossomed later."

Anne laughed. The remark struck a chord of disbelief, and a wry smile played a moment on her full mouth. It would appear, she thought, that not everyone was in agreement. The thought of Mr. Blakewell would not spoil her day. Tossing her head, she said, "I'll race you when we reach the meadow."

Seth Blakewell was about to spoil many days to come. He was seated on horseback en route to Surrey. He had decided after Lord and Lady Rothier's ball to leave immediately to call upon his grandfather. He planned to arrive unannounced. Then he could demand an audience. Catching them unaware might just be the lever to the success of this mission.

Comfortably dressed in his soft, fringed buckskins,

traveling the rutted road on so brilliant a day, Seth felt a rising optimism. The conclusion of what he had originally come to England for seemed to be within his grasp.

He mulled over the situation, vowing to clear his father's name and claim the lady. It would be no easy task; he risked much. If only he could keep the information of his father's betrayal couched in mild terms, without divulging the sordid events . . . His grandfather need not know every detail.

If he were successful, he might put himself in the position to at least demand permission to seek Annemarie's hand. He was positive he could entrap her father into a situation wherein Marshall would have to concede him the right. His conscience, which reminded him that this was little better than blackmail, bothered him not at all. Marshall deserved no quarter, nor did Cecil. He would bring pressure on Cecil to get Anthony to withdraw. Cecil would have to agree or risk exposure. Seth smiled with the satisfaction of an infallible scheme.

If the lady in question were to learn of his subterfuge, he knew she would react with fierce indignation, perhaps come to hate him. Miss Marshall was no mild, submissive lady and she would refuse him out of hand. He would have to exert great care that she did not learn of her father's involvement. He could not bear the thought of her pain if that were to happen.

He would just have to be vigilant to avoid the facts becoming known. Neither Marshall nor Cecil would freely volunteer disclosing their part in a plot of betrayal and attempted murder, so Seth felt safe. He would carry it off.

9

The autumn beauty of the terrain through which he traveled brought thoughts of Georgia to Seth's mind. Georgia, with its lush green live oak and hanging Spanish moss, never sported such a multitude of vivid autumn hues, but the changing leaves were enough to bring a sparkling image of home.

He admired the picturesque, well-kept, rolling land through which he passed, knowing it represented centuries of cultivation. The contrasting image of the untouched wilderness brought an urgent desire to complete this mission and leave this confining land. The glorious day brought a longing to traipse the wilderness again, and the realization that he would now be hunting in the mountains if he were home.

Approaching the Sutton land, he thought of the time they had come down from London to buy horses. He had first seen Miss Marshall then. Her image brought a thrill reverberating through his body. She didn't belong among the simpering ladies of London. She belonged beside him, taming the new land. Somehow, somehow he must see that she did not marry his cousin Anthony. Tightening his gloved hands on the reins, he set his mind from the tawny-eyed lady and spurred his horse to a faster pace and the gates of Chathram Manor.

Passing through the stone gates, he cantered down the park

lane, coming upon the clearing of sweeping lawns that ran up to the manor house. Ornamental fountains were spraying glistening patterns on the water in the enormous rectangular pool. The clever design was brilliant and successfully executed to reflect the magnificent house. The reflection gave an Elysian quality to the approaching traveler.

Pausing a moment, Seth tried to imagine his father brought up in such a magnificent scene. He could not. In his mind's eye, he saw his father wearing buckskins and coming into the house, his hunting dogs yapping at his heels. Viewing such splendid surroundings, it was easier to understand why his father had been quiet and dignified.

The monumental house was intimidating. Seth straightened his back and urged his stallion forward, as if into battle.

The moment he reached the curved drive before the entrance, a young boy appeared from alongside the path to take his horse. The freckled-faced youth stared in awe at the fringed buckskin attire this stranger sported.

"Thank you, lad," Seth said as he dismounted. "Please see that the horse is brushed down and given something to eat." He flipped a coin into the the lad's hand, to the great delight of the youngster. Such largesse did not come his way often. It must be because he is a foreigner, the boy thought as he led the fine stallion around to the stable.

Seth swiftly mounted the steps of the well-proportioned manor. To his surprise, the door opened as he raised his hand to pull the bell chain. A liveried footman stood in the opened door with an expression of amazement at the roughly dressed stranger. Seth stepped forward, brushing past the speechless servant.

The interior had the intended, overwhelming effect on Seth—perhaps more so, for he had never seen anything so monumental and beautiful in his life. He stood, arrested by the magnificence of the hall, until he noticed the haughty butler crossing the vast expanse toward him. A flicker crossed his eyes as they narrowed. He had deliberately worn his frontier riding clothes to proclaim the unmistakable identity of who he was. How incongruous to the interior he appeared, and the thought annoyed him.

Wilkins, the butler, was horrified. This tall, extraordinary, formidable-looking man who stood with a somehow foreboding expression was doubtless no gentleman. He sniffed, an obvious look of disapproval upon his long, pointed face.

Seth's momentary discomfiture at his dress faded. He smiled slightly. It was not a smile, precisely, but a grimace that seemed to slit his face, displaying his even white teeth and giving a menacing expression, thus creating the disturbing effect he so desired.

"Tell the Earl of Chathram Seth Blakewell of Georgia wishes to see him," Seth drawled in a low, commanding voice.

"I'm not sure his lordship is in to receive visitors," Wilkins replied with the hauteur of a king and an emphasis on the word *visitors*.

"He'll see me," Seth said, stepping closer to the butler.

Wilkins stepped back and flushed. With exaggerated slowness, the butler crossed the hall to mount the stairs to the first floor.

Seth stood and watched the man with interest. His exact counterpart did not exist in America. At least he knew of none.

The wait seemed to last forever while Seth was left to cool his heels. Knowing he'd been rudely delegated to stand in the hall rather than given a seat in one of the rooms off the foyer, he shifted uneasily. The splendor of the magnificent surroundings overpowered his confidence. Frowning with an ill-at-ease feeling, Seth started to move to the stairs. His grandfather would see him, by God, he would!

At that moment, Wilkins emerged at the top of the sweeping staircase. From this lofty position and with undisguised pleasure he said, "The Earl of Chathram is not receiving visitors. I'll see that your horse is brought around immediately."

Wilkins started to descend the steps just as Seth crossed the hall and began to mount them. "Return to the earl and tell him his grandson from America is here to see him," Seth ordered.

Stunned, the butler stood rooted. "As you wish," Wilkins finally said, but he was visibly surprised.

Seth remained with one booted foot on the step, looking for all the world as if he were about to pounce.

This time the butler scurried like a rabbit down the hall to the master's sitting room.

Breathlessly entering the room, Wilkins blurted, "He says he is your grandson and insists on seeing you!"

The earl slowly rose, his eyes wide with disbelief. He weighed the information. "Put him in the library. I shall be there in a moment," he finally said.

Escorted into the library off the lower hall, Seth stood at the window watching the fountains on the front lawn. Anger at his father's family and the condescending attitude of the servants sent a rod-of-steel determination through his body. With his hands behind his back and his legs slightly parted, he appeared every inch the resolute man he was. Seth turned at the sound of the opening door and watched the elderly gentleman slowly enter the room. Seth stared with unabashed interest.

The old earl looked incredibly like his father. Seth felt a rush of unnamed emotion. The earl was tall, with abundant white hair. His body was erect, his keen blue eyes alert with incredulous interest. Seth was pleased to see he was in apparent good health.

Lord Chathram paused a moment, taking in this dark-haired stranger. He continued into the room, his eyes searching Seth's face. He could find no family resemblance, except, perhaps, in demeanor.

"My butler informs me that you claim to be a grandson of mine. Will you be so kind as to explain yourself?" Chathram moved slowly closer.

With a swift stride, Seth turned and closed the space between them. "I had wished to introduce that fact privately, but this is apparently the only way I could get to see you. As you know, my first request, by letter, was turned down. It seems I had no other option. I find my father's family decidedly lacking in at least the rudiments of familial interest."

Chathram continued to take his measure. "Be seated and explain your claim. I have received no previous request from you," the earl said, taking a seat himself and indicating Seth to do likewise in the chair opposite him.

"Mr. Addison sent my request, and it was turned down, as well you know."

A perceivable frown marked the earl's lined face. *That is easy enough to verify,* the elderly gentleman thought. The implications, if it proved to be true, brought a deepening frown to his face.

Seth responded to the frown on the earl's face by leaning forward in his chair. "I am here at the bequest of my mother. It is not to my liking, I assure you. I would not have chosen to have come to you. My mother's wishes supersede my own. The grasping evil of this family is nothing I would wish to claim. Despite your lack of interest, I will inform you that John did indeed live, and successfully so. Like me, he never wished to see his family again," Seth said with direct harshness.

Chathram looked as though he had been slapped. His eyes traveled to Seth's hand, and he saw the signet ring. "You say John is alive? Where did you get the ring?"

"My father died this year of the fever. The ring was his," Seth replied, and sat back in his chair. He was suddenly sorry he had spoken so harshly. His grandfather was an old man and deserved politeness even if he had not yet earned his respect.

"Tell me your story," the earl said in a quiet restrained voice.

"I'm not sure how much I wish to tell you. It will not bring you much pleasure, for the duplicity of your family is a lineage to Cain and Abel," Seth said. He made no attempt to hide the disdain he held for the Blakewells.

"Your son, John, survived the journey and landed in Savannah. He met and married Alma Sorenson. Alma is the daughter of a fine Swede who started a plantation outside of Savannah. Her mother was a full-blooded Creek Indian, a daughter of a chief. So, I am part American Indian, and I know with what distaste you hold foreigners; that should rankle a bit more. Believe me, it is not we who are savages."

The Earl of Chathram sat quietly and did not comment.

Seth continued, "Upon my father's death my mother beseeched me to come to England to clear my father's name. He did not shoot young Williamson in that argument. You see, the Creek nation has a very valued opinion on the honor a man holds. My mother will not rest until she knows my father's name is cleared, for he was a most honorable man. It was not he who dishonored this family."

Chathram winced. "We are a family of honor. You will not malign it again. I do not know you are my grandson merely because you wear my son's ring. It could have been stolen or any such thing. You will refrain from your derisive language or you may leave this instant.''

Seth smiled with admiration. He liked the truthful bluntness of the old man. Therefore, he nodded in agreement.

Chathram perceived his change as respect and nodded in return accord. ''You seriously lack manners, young man. Why are you here? Is it money or the inheritance that would be due you if your story is true?'' the old earl said with continued bluntness. He had decided it was something the young American understood.

Seth had expected just such a reaction, and a derisive smile hovered over his lips. He leveled his eyes on the earl and said, ''I am considered a wealthy man in America. I own Riverview, which is the plantation that my parents built together. I own three sailing vessels and have made a vast profit in shipping due to the politics of our respective countries. I don't need or want your money.''

''You take advantage of the embargoes? It seems you can bend your honor at will, Creek or otherwise,'' Chathram shrewdly replied.

With that quick-witted response, Seth cocked an eyebrow, and his estimation of the old gentleman soared. A twinkle entered his eyes. The frank speech pleased Seth. It dawned on him that the old gentleman knew nothing of his earlier request to see him.

''I have my father's papers. I want you to see them, and I will tell you about him, if you so wish. Then I shall return to America, having accomplished my mother's mission.''

''Will you remain with me for a short while? This is overwhelming news. I am sure to have questions to ask you later, and if you have gone, my opportunity will have passed. If what you say is true, you cannot object to my request,'' Lord Blakewell said.

''Agreed! I shall spend some time with you. You would

have been proud of John. I know a man never had a finer father," Seth said, his voice choked with emotion.

"I was always proud of John. It broke my heart when he shot a man over cards and had to leave the country a step ahead of the magistrates," Chathram said, starting to slowly rise from his chair.

Seth rose at the same time, understanding the interview was over. "Well, you can rest easy. It was not John. He was blameless," Seth added.

The Earl of Chathram stood a moment and looked at the rough-hewn American. He made no reply.

They walked to the door and Lord Blakewell turned and asked, "The costume you wear is meant to intimidate or set you apart?"

Seth laughed softly. The wily old man, he thought. "To impress," he replied.

The Earl of Chathram chuckled softly.

As they entered the hall, Wilkins was nonchalantly standing a short distance from the door, looking for all the world as if the magnificent ceiling he was examining was something he had never seen before. Chathram frowned; he knew the nosy old retainer had had his ear pressed to the door.

"Wilkins, see that Mr. Blakewell is settled into a guest room. He will be staying a few days." He turned to Seth. "Now, you must excuse me. I will see you at dinner. Feel free to make yourself comfortable. There is an excellent library and stable." He gave a slight bow and left Seth to the care of a thoroughly amazed Wilkins.

10

With an irritated gesture, Annemarie snapped the book closed. Too distracted to concentrate on the book, she sighed. Restlessly she stretched her hands over her head as if the movement would relieve her boredom. The inactivity was oppressive; she felt she would soon suffocate in London. Knowing she was out of sorts, she also realized she could do nothing to change it.

Rising, she walked to the window and stared out onto the nearly empty street. What rankled most was understanding she had been content when she held the hopes of seeing Mr. Blakewell again. Now that that hope seemed to be gone, the excitement of London faded as fast as the illusive American. This, above all, set her spirits at low ebb. There was her pride and the vague sense of rejection that haunted her. He had seemed interested in furthering their acquaintance. She blushed at the thought. Her actions were those of a silly schoolgirl. How foolish! She knew little about him. Why should she be so vexed? Surely it wasn't just a manly form that could set her pulses racing, she reasoned. It simply did not make sense. The best thing to do was firmly put him out of her thoughts, but it seemed that was easier said than done. Her morbid thoughts were interrupted when the butler announced Lord Anthony Blakewell wished to see her.

Anthony had called often of late, and this pleased her, since she enjoyed his humor. He was a good diversion, she thought guiltily, knowing one shouldn't consider a friendship in such a self-serving manner.

Lord Anthony entered the parlor with a weak smile upon his lips and a strained expression in his eyes.

"Good morning, Anthony," Anne said with as much cheerfulness as she could muster.

"Greetings, Anne. You are dazzling. I declare, London does suit you."

A soft laugh escaped from her lips. "You are good for me this morning. My humor is totally lacking, and I wish I were back at Sutton Hall," she said.

Anthony looked into her tawny-green eyes and saw the sadness in them. He frowned. "Dear friend," he said, placing a hand on her shoulder, "I see you are indeed out of sorts. Let's go riding as soon as I have seen your father. That should cheer you up."

Anne examined his red-rimmed blue eyes and found a genuine concern. She smiled, but distress tugged at her heart. Seeing the unhealthy pallor and the tired eyes, she realized he must be persuaded from his present pursuit of the temptations of London. But how? she wondered.

"See my father? Whatever for?" she hastily asked.

He shrugged. "I'll inform you as soon as I know," he replied, knowing quite well the reason, but reluctant to say so at this moment.

Lord Anthony had called on several occasions recently to see Anne. Caroline had fawned over him to the point of embarrassment, and this had placed Anne at even greater odds with her mother. Anne was not pleased with the implication she read in her mother's actions.

During these visits Sissy had smiled in encouragement and empathy toward her niece, positive Anne had been intrigued by the tall American. So, Sissy had tried to add her cheerful chatter and distracting ideas in order to soften what, she was certain, was a hurt carried by Annemarie. Sissy also wondered at Caroline's apparent blindness to her own daughter's unhappiness.

Quentin decided to speak with Anthony and suggest he declare for Annemarie. For this reason the young man now stood in the front parlor with Annemarie.

The moment of understanding friendship was interrupted by Jenkins, informing them that Lord Anthony was required in Lord Sutton's study by Squire Marshall.

Anthony gave Anne a squeeze on her shoulder and smiled. "Wait for me. I'll take you riding after we have finished," he said as he squared his shoulders and left the room.

Anthony's small movement was not lost on Anne and she stood silent. Her heart began to race. A dawning idea gave her immediate discomfort. Surely not yet, she thought. Deep down she knew full well: she would have an offer from Anthony, and her parents would insist she accept. Her spirits sank even lower. She left the room in order to change into her riding habit.

Anne was correct in her assessment of the topic of conversation between Lord Anthony and her father.

"I think it is time you speak to Annemarie. She seems so restless in London, and the announced engagement will keep her busy with wedding plans. We plan to have a ball to make the announcement," Quentin said, seating himself comfortably in the leather wing chair. He had wasted no time in coming to the subject.

Lord Anthony cringed at the directness of the squire. He didn't want a wife now. Least of all did he want to be allied to Quentin and Caroline Marshall. By God, he thought, they'll not see much of me if I do marry Anne. He had not yet accepted this fate.

"I'm not sure Anne will accept me. Perhaps we should

wait a while longer," Anthony replied, crossing his elegant booted legs and brushing imaginary flecks of lint from his tight buff breeches.

"No, she will consent. I wish you to ask her. It would be best if she feels it is what you desire, rather than what her parents want. She will be more pleased if you do so. I think we should get on with it. She is bored with London and this will keep her busy. Women have a way of making a simple wedding a major event." Squire Marshall chuckled. His weak attempt at humor only managed to annoy.

"My father agrees," Anthony said. He could think of nothing else to add. It all seemed to be closing in on him. He knew he had no choice. He was trapped.

"Buck up, my boy!" Quentin laughed. "There's not a man alive that doesn't come to marriage without trepidation. Annemarie loves the country. I think she'll not come up to London often. You'll have the freedom you desire."

Lord Anthony had the grace to be horrified that such a remark could come from Anne's father. His estimation of the man was further lowered. Maybe he's correct, Anthony selfishly agreed, not recognizing his own duplicity, or at least softening it by the fact Annemarie might well be better off with him and at Chathram Manor.

"Anne and I are about to go riding. I'll ask her then," he said with resignation. He rose to leave.

"I'll discuss the marriage contract with your father," Marshall said.

Anthony nodded with a fierce glance. I'll just bet you will—and make it to your advantage, he thought.

Moments later, the young couple was seated on their fine horses and carefully making their way through the streets toward Green Park. Little conversation passed between them. Both were lost, deep in their own thoughts.

Entering the park, Anne beheld the beauty of the trees and

the golden leaves scattered along the grass and paths. The view was so enchanting Anne felt a surge of elation.

"It's a golden world today, Tony. Remember when we were children and piled the leaves high so we could jump into them?" she asked.

Anthony returned the smile. He thought she was stylish in her topaz velvet habit, but he remembered the girl. "You've always been a bit of a golden girl yourself," he said.

"My, what a compliment. At least, I take it as such."

"It was meant as such. Anne, we've been friends for all our days. It would please our parents if we were to marry. Would you do me the honor of becoming my wife?" he asked.

Anne laughed. "Proposed to on a horse."

"I could think of no other place you'd rather be," he teased.

"You're probably right," she said with a sudden seriousness to her voice. "Do you really wish to wed? And am I your honest choice? I hear the commands of your father behind the offer."

"Annemarie, you always manage to speak to the point. You are correct. My father thinks I must wed, to settle me down. I can think of no other with whom I feel so easy."

"True, but that is because of our long-standing friendship. Is it what you want? I agree we would probably get on well. However, I do not approve of your gambling or the other tales I hear," she gravely added.

He glanced over to her. A silence fell between them.

"You'd have to change all that, Tony, for your own good," she added.

"You sound like a wife already and refine too much on what is rumor. Yes, I've gambled some, but not to excess.

I will be the model husband with such a capable lady at my side," he finally said, but his voice was flat.

They rode on for a while. "This is the most unusual proposal, Tony."

He cast her an inquiring look. "What of you? Is it what you would wish? Do you not want a dashing knight in armor to declare his undying love at your feet? I thought all ladies hope for that sort of thing."

"I don't believe many people have such matches. Just look around at the people we know. How many have a love match? We probably would have a better chance than most. We like each other. You will have to give up your bachelor life in town," she said, guiding her horse out into an open meadow. "I'll race you."

Laughing together, they rode with spirit, ending at the far end of the meadow, where they brought their horses to a halt. For a few moments they sat their horses in silence.

The handsome young pair in deep concentration with the golden leaves fluttering down made an appealing picture for any passerby.

"Well, my dear, do we make a match?" Anthony said at last.

She raised her eyes to his. For one split second a pair of smoky gray-green eyes flashed in her mind's eye. Shifting on her saddle, she nodded. "Yes, Tony, we'll make a good match. I will be your wife, and I am honored you asked me."

Anthony bit his lower lip a second and gazed up at the blue sky. He moved his horse forward. "Come, we must return and tell your family. They want to give you an engagement ball. How about a spring wedding?" he asked.

Anne maneuvered her horse next to his. "Could we consider the ball at Chathram Manor? We could make the announcement during the hunt ball. It would save an extra expense, since the hunt ball is given every year. Please, Tony. I'm mad to get back to Surrey and my horses."

"You make Surrey sound a thousand miles away, instead of a few miles." He laughed.

"It might as well be," she said.

"I'll speak to grandfather and tell him we wish to make our betrothal announcement at the hunt ball. Now, he is someone who will rejoice. Grandfather loves you. He will tell me I don't deserve you by half, and maybe he's right."

"Oh, Tony! We'll do just fine. You'll see. At any rate, we will be free of parents nagging at us," she teased.

"The thought is infinitely appealing," he said, laughing in return.

They headed their horses homeward, the matter settled.

Caroline was sitting with Sissy when Lord Anthony and Anne returned to the Sutton town house. They entered the parlor with an air of expectancy. Sissy perceived it instantly, and a slight frown crossed her eyes. She watched Anne's face in apprehension.

"Mrs. Marshall, Lady Sutton, I am pleased to tell you that Anne has done me the honor of accepting my proposal of marriage," Lord Anthony said in stilted tones, as if he had rehearsed the speech.

Caroline rose with a squeal of delight. She hugged her daughter. "How wonderful! We are so fond of you, Lord Anthony. It will be a very happy union. You are so well-acquainted," she gushed.

Anne's eyes traveled to Sissy's and saw the question in them, and she dropped her gaze. Her heart began to pound.

Sissy slowly rose and smiled. "I'm so happy for you both," she said, hoping against hope her niece was not making a mistake.

"Anne wishes to make the announcement during the hunt ball at Chathram Manor. We hope that is agreeable," Anthony said.

Caroline was surprised. "That is only two weeks away. I'm aware the invitations are already sent, since we have received ours. There are those whom I should like to invite. And she'll need a new gown," Caroline complained.

"You can invite anyone you might wish. Anne is beautiful in whatever she might wear. I wish to please her on this account. I'm sure you can accommodate me in this matter," Anthony said as he reached and took Anne's hand.

Caroline was a bit taken aback by his forceful manner.

"Well, of course, if that is what you both desire. but it seems a bit hurried to me," she said with a slight plaintive whine in her voice. "When do you plan the wedding?"

Lord Anthony looked to Anne.

"In the spring, Mother. There is enough time to make those plans," Anne answered.

Sissy moved to take her niece's hand. "We'll have a gown made, and the hunt ball will be a lovely time to make the announcement."

Lord Anthony managed to smile, despite the overwhelming desire to escape the fawning Mrs. Marshall. He informed Anne he would accompany her to the ball given by Lady Holland that evening, made his excuses, and took his leave. Placing his hat on his head, he paused a moment on the step. The die was cast, he thought. Well, Anne was tolerable, but it would be a good thing he would not have to see much of that harridan who would be his mother-in-law.

Anne made her escape as soon as she was able to do so. Slowly stretching out on her bed, she closed her eyes. Would she live to regret her actions? Did she already? There seemed to be little other option open to her. She had no dowry to speak of, no outstanding family connections, and no legion of suitors. Tony was agreeable. *Agreeable,* what a pallid word, she thought. She wasn't in love with him. She did not approve of his idle existence, nor of his gaming pursuits. Perhaps that will all change when he is a family man. Tears welled in her eyes. Oh, if only . . . But that could not be. Even if the elusive Mr. Blakewell had pursued her, would she have ever left England with him? She didn't even know who he was or what he believed in. It was just that she had thought she could read so much in his misty eyes. She had been wrong.

A tear rolled down her cheek. Romantic unions existed only in stories and novels. Since she had no choice, she would have to make the best of it. Anthony was a friend, and she loved Chathram Manor. She would have her horses and could content herself in the country once again. She brightened at the prospect. All would be well; she would make it so.

Dinner was a happy affair. Quentin and Caroline were in high spirits. Anthony was expected later to escort her to the evening's entertainment. Devon watched with interest, delighted for his niece.

Quentin rose to make an elaborate toast to Anne's good fortune. "To Annemarie," he said, raising his glass, "our fortunate daughter, who has received an offer from Lord Blakewell. May this advantageous marriage prove to be the happy union I expect it to be."

Anne frowned; he made it sound as if she were some antidote, barely able to get an offer. The implication annoyed her. She kept her eyes on the food set before her, entering little in the buoyant festivities of her father.

Marshall's high spirits and effusive manner were also partially due to his secret planning of an outstanding business venture. None of the family was aware he planned to spend the next morning looking at a site for a new dock. Angus Grey had explained the singular opportunity that was to be had. Mr. Blakewell was currently seeking the investors who would finance the venture. It was sure to be a resounding success. It couldn't fail. Quentin had at last found the investment he had dreamed of all his life. There was a chance Devon or Cecil would lend him money, or perhaps he would mortgage Sutton Manor. But no matter, he would be a part of this great opportunity.

"Let us drink to all our good fortune," Quentin said, once again raising his glass. The red wine sloshed over the edge.

"Quentin, do be careful. You've had quite enough," Caroline admonished.

Anne sat very still, awaiting the explosion of wrath from her father. He did not tolerate directions issued in front of others. To her surprise he laughed.

"My dear, allow me a little merriment. Besides Anne's good fortune, I've been in some discussion with Mr. Grey on a very profitable business opportunity. So bid me no prattle on curbing my toasts. Tonight there is reason to celebrate," he said.

Anne's head snapped up. "Mr. Grey? Is Mr. Blakewell in the venture also?" Anne caught Sissy's gaze on her and dropped her eyes, a blush stealing up her face.

"Certainly, none of this could be of interest to you ladies. Mr. Blakewell is away on business, but I assure you we have his expertise to guide us," Quentin said, regretting his lapse in mentioning the matter. He realized, instantly, his wine had loosened his tongue.

"You better investigate his background before you invest," Devon cautioned.

Quentin's hand slammed down on the table. He rose, somewhat unsteady. "Enough! The conversation is not of interest to any of you. It is just an idea. It may never come about,'' he lied, giving a weaving bow and mustering what dignity he could to leave the room.

The remaining diners sat in silence. Caroline's face was scarlet. "Whatever did you question your father for?" she hotly asked her daughter.

Anne looked surprised. "It's not my—"

Sissy placed a hand on Caroline's arm. "Think nothing of it. He is just slightly overwhelmed with the good news and all. Everything will be forgotten in moments," she kindly said.

Devon stood. He was as annoyed as could be possible. Damn, he thought, this is my house. I'll not have this again at my dinner table. He shot Sissy a quelling look. She nodded in understanding. "Let us retire to prepare for the evening's events," he said.

Anne was aghast, and if she had been upset with the absent Mr. Blakewell before, she was now enraged at him, faulting him for grievances unknown. If she never saw him again, it would be too soon.

11

The days spent with the Earl of Chathram presented Seth with mixed feelings. He could not help but be impressed with the enormous, well-run manor. The grounds were beautifully kept, the stables housed some of the finest horses Seth had ever seen, and the library held a collection that had taken hundreds of years to acquire.

Seth was disarmed by the forthright earl, who reminded him of his father. It was easy to imagine just how his father would have been in later life. Seth told Lord Blakewell that during their first long conversation. The earl refrained from comment as they sat in the comfortable library.

The room was large and well-lighted from the tall, mullioned windows at both ends. In it, one had the feeling of timeless stability. The warm wood paneling and large Tudor fireplace added to the sense of comfort and encouraged intimate conversation.

Lord Blakewell scrutinized the tall American in veiled observance. He still could find no family resemblance in the exotic quality of his dark hair and high cheekbones. Lord Blakewell could see the young man was confident and assured. He liked that.

"Please tell me your story. I do not think you have come so far for so little reason," Lord Blakewell finally requested.

Seth smiled. "You are correct. I can see how my father's

life might have been, had events not changed the course of his life. I am convinced he eventually came to love his American life more than that of his native land. He was a fine man and deserves the exculpation of his name.''

"That would please me, if I could believe it were so.''

"I know that my father was innocent. Therefore, I will tell you my father did not do the shooting. He was betrayed. The detailed events of his betrayal need not be discussed. He chose to give up his family connections rather than cause the pain of such a disclosure. I ask you to trust the truth of these words.''

The earl sat quietly listening as Seth continued. "During his escape from England, his life was at peril, and the captain of the ship allowed him to jump ship at Savannah. You will remember, Savannah was still under British control at that time.''

"If you do not give me all the information, how am I to believe?'' Lord Blakewell said.

Seth paused a moment as he considered this point. "There is no reason to bring more sorrow when my intention is to carry out my mother's request. Let me tell you about his life and family. I have already mentioned he married Alma Sorenson. You might be interested to know, Mother was the granddaughter of a Creek chief, and since inheritance passes through the mother's side of the family, unlike the English, I could have claimed that right,'' Seth said, and watched his grandfather for a reaction. None was forthcoming.

Seth arched his black eyebrows. "You surprise me, sir. I had expected a reaction of horror to find your grandson is part Indian,'' Seth said.

"I do not know you are my grandson.''

Seth smiled derisively. "Yes, I can see that would be the only reason you are not shocked,'' he said.

"You make far too many assumptions. You are impertinent

and do not know what I believe or do not believe. You seem bent on announcing the fact you are of Indian descent on every occasion, as if to judge a man by his reaction. I question your motive. Please continue,'' Lord Blakewell said.

Seth was taken aback by the stinging truth of the earl's words. The rebuke was justified and Seth realized he was guilty of his own prejudice.

Justly humbled, Seth continued. ''After my father's death, my mother requested I come to see if you still lived. She wanted you to know that Father was innocent and that he always loved you,'' Seth said with a catch in his low voice.

The old earl shuddered a moment. ''He could have written. In fact, I hold my son would never have allowed me to think he was dead all these years,'' he said with an edge of bitterness in his voice.

''He was not willing to have you suffer on two accounts. The betrayal was too deep. He wanted no more of such a family, but he regretted that you did not know he survived and made a happy life for himself.''

Seth went on to tell him of John's life in America; the plantation and his noble mother, who worked side by side with her husband in the development of the plantation from a wilderness.

''What is it you wish?'' the earl finally asked.

''Nothing, absolutely nothing from this family, I assure you. I have brought my message.''

Seth took out his leather pouch and handed his father's papers to Lord Blakewell. The elderly gentleman adjusted his spectacles and carefully examined them.

''They are his papers. They could have been acquired any number of ways,'' he said.

Seth nodded. ''He told me once when he was young that you and he were caught in a snowstorm while hunting. He used to laugh when he remembered the story. He said you both found shelter in an abandoned hut. You gathered wood, cooked the rabbit over a smoky fire, and spent the night before the weather cleared, allowing you to return. He always said it was his first lesson in survival, and inadvertently a lesson for his life on the frontier. I can now see why the incident always amused him; the great Earl of Chathram taught him that first lesson. He said you would have made it anywhere, since you were a man of ability, not a mincing fop who seems to abound among the idle aristocrats. I did not then know you were an earl, for he never spoke of it.''

The earl looked surprised at the remembered incident, but he realized it could have been repeated by anyone. ''Did he tell you anything else?''

''Yes, many stories. He told me that evening he had cried, and you said that a man need not cry if he had the ability to change a situation,'' Seth replied.

His grandfather sat quietly, his expression bleak; a weariness showed in the slight slump of his shoulders. He had asked Seth to remain a few days and during that time they passed many hours in conversation about his father's life.

When at last Seth was ready to leave, the earl spoke to him with reserved approval. ''I do not know what to make of all that you have told me during your stay. Many of the events only John could have known. I want time to consider all you have said. Will you return to see me? We are famous for our excellent hunting. Please join us at the hunt we hold every year. You may not be interested in the ball or riding to the hounds, but I promise you great hunting. You probably will excel with your wilderness experience. My, how that will rankle some of the pompous guests!'' Lord Blakewell chuckled. The earl wanted the time to investigate the missing request sent by James Addison.

Seth instantly seized the opportunity. He thought of Miss Marshall, knowing she would in all probability be attending. In fact, he spent far too many moments thinking of that young lady. The invitation presented a chance to be with her, and he could not refuse. "I should like that very much. I accept," Seth said eagerly as he swung up on his horse.

The earl was standing on the steps of the front portico to bid the American farewell. He looked frail, and it was a mark of honor that he had chosen to escort his guest to the place of his departure. The earl was a bit surprised at his swift reply. He frowned a moment; perhaps he is seeking something, after all. Well, the hunt would be a good opportunity to find out.

They parted on friendly terms, but the Earl of Chathram was not convinced of his identity. He liked the young man well enough, but too many facts remained unanswered for him to be convinced this man was his grandson. He knew too well the meaning behind the hidden implications of Seth's story and did not yet want to accept them. Still, he could not deny the ring of truth in them.

Seth returned to London. Angus Grey and Seth diligently began to carry out the plan they had decided would best accomplish their purposes.

They took Squire Marshall to see the land along the Thames below Surrey Docks on the South Bank. Enclosed docks were in high demand, and a dock thus placed would be most advantageous. Being a man of law, Angus had enough education to understand English law and the knowledge of legal references to properly impress the country squire.

Seth was amused by Angus as he watched the smooth

"country" lawyer press the squire with seemingly innocent charm.

They stood looking at the heavy traffic of shipping vessels of every description.

"You can see for yourself, another dock could be only a great success," Angus said.

Marshall nodded as he observed the busy scene. "You're absolutely correct. Can the money be raised?"

"We have the monies. It is going to take most of our capital, and another investor would be desirable, but not necessary," Seth lied.

"I would like to join in the venture, but my funds are tied up for the most part," Marshall said with a pronounced regret. He knew he had spoiled his chances by speaking too soon the previous evening. He could not approach Devon for the money.

"Why don't you mortgage some of your land and come into the venture? You'll double your investment in a year following completion," Angus suggested.

"I'd never consider that," Quentin said. He knew Caroline would cause such a ruckus he'd not have a moment's peace, and Lord Sutton would back her up. Such an action, if discovered, would create a havoc that his life wouldn't be worth a tinker's damn. He sighed. What a golden opportunity! he thought, the one I have waited for all my life.

"That is understandable. Unfortunately, we just have to let some opportunities pass. Well, shall we go?" Angus said, and turned to leave the river's edge.

"Would you take a pledge of money? A personal note? I could put up land, but it would have to be a private agreement . . . you understand. My wife . . ." Quentin said, and allowed his words to trail away.

"Of course, I understand. Ladies simply have no understanding of financial matters. A note would be advantageous to us, for it would show the bankers we have ample funds for the project. Yes, a promissory note would be acceptable. I'm sure you will agree Mr. Grey,'' Seth said.

Angus nodded gravely.

''It can only help us to have a gentleman of your standing among our numbers, considering we are not well-known in your country. So we all benefit,'' Seth said, shaking hands to seal the bargain.

Quentin Marshall was elated to be in the venture. He knew it was sound. Never had he had such a promising chance for a fortune! A weak smile hovered on his lips. Caroline must not discover that he had mortgaged Sutton Hall until it was a success, he thought.

The gentlemen then parted company.

The two Americans spent that evening in Lord Charling's company, continuing to carry out their plan. Angus was to inform Lord Charling that they had arranged all the financing for the new docks to be built.

They were leaving the Westminster Dog Pit in Torhill Fields after viewing an Italian monkey fighting a dog twice his weight for a hundred-guinea purse. Both Seth and Angus were amazed to learn the dog was owned by a nobleman, and they were even more astounded at the fervor of the audience.

''Mere blades all anxious to sport their blunt,'' Charling explained.

Seth shook his head and shrugged. ''You'd think they'd bet on something with better odds and far greater returns.''

As anticipated, Charling was immediately interested in the remark. ''What do you mean?'' he asked.

''Well, this must remain confidential, but we are impressed with the financial opportunity of the vastly needed docks on the Thames. It is beyond any we have encountered. We're going to build the best covered and walled dock on the river. We have most of our venture money. 'Tis a gamble better than any turn of the card or quirk of fate in the agility of a monkey,'' Angus explained.

"Where would you get that much money? It would take a bloody fortune! Besides, gentlemen do not deal in commerce,'' Charling added with a sneer of hauteur.

"You're sadly mistaken. They merely don't admit to it. How do you think some of the noblemen keep up their extravagant living? They engage in business behind the scenes without their names being known. Clever lot, they are,'' Seth said.

Lord Charling sighed; he constantly struggled to make ends meet. He gambled and cheated young men in order to keep himself out of Newgate. Funds seldom remained with him long. Lady Luck was far too capricious.

"Would you allow me to invest? Discreetly, of course,'' he said, glancing left and right, as if someone might be listening.

Vastly amused, Angus turned, feigning surprise. "You would wish to enter a commercial enterprise?''

Lord Charling reluctantly nodded, wondering where in the devil he could raise the money. He had an evening planned with Lord Anthony Blakewell. He had carefully nurtured the young man for weeks. Tonight he would take him for all he could.

"Let me speak to my man of business. Will you give me a day or two to see if I might be able to join in this undertaking?'' Lord Charling lied, prompted by the perennial optimism of the seasoned gambler.

"Actually, we are fully funded, but it is the wise businessman with extra capital for unexpected problems who succeeds.''

"Indeed, but I would not wish my name connected to it," Lord Charling cautioned.

"English ways are foreign to me. Can't see why a man wouldn't be proud to be known as a wise businessman. In America it's a mark of achievement. If you choose to invest, we will not let that fact be known," Seth said, then thought to himself. If we were really going to build a dock, it would be best to not have a rogue such as Charling as an investor. His gambling reputation was far too well-known.

When they parted, Angus gave Seth a pat on the shoulder, pleased with their day's work. So two very satisfied conspirators returned to the Portland Place mansion.

12

The news of Young Anthony Blakewell's staggering loss of over ten thousand pounds in a game of rouleaux was repeated in detail by Angus during breakfast early the next morning.

"Young Anthony was foxed. Charling plied the young fool with wine all evening, patiently drawing him in with small losses and some wins, but the last throw was his object. Charling doubled the stakes in the last roll. He made it seem an offhanded offer, and I'm not even sure Lord Anthony was aware of it," Angus explained.

Seth listened with interest to the events that would place Anthony within his grasp.

"A hush fell over the room when Charling threw, and the dice came up cinque-ace. Hard to believe such luck, and judging from the gasp of the gathered observers, few could. Phenomenal luck? Unlikely . . . I'd stake a pretty purse that they were rigged."

Angus shrugged and continued. "Young Blakewell was devastated. There was mass confusion, I thought for a minute there might be a fight. A friend took Lord Blakewell home. We were all more than a little concerned that he might do harm to himself. A devilish business. I can't understand the fascination of gaming. But be assured, Charling's reputation is further dimished. After all, Lord Anthony is little more than a callow youth," Angus said.

Seth felt a rush of regret. He should be pleased, since it was exactly what he had hoped would happen. Instead, his conscience bothered him. The damn fool, he thought, knowing full well it was his deliberate goading of Charling to invest that had instigated the fateful game. He may have acted behind the scene, and it was those actions that brought about Anthony's downfall.

Seth spent little time in consideration of Lord Anthony's own choice in entering the foolhardy game. Now that he had Lord Anthony where he wanted him, he wondered if he was right. He cared what his grandfather thought.

Angus watched the pained expression on Seth's face and understood his friend's ambivalence.

"Seth, it will work, you'll bring it around," Angus encouraged.

"Then best I be about doing so," Seth replied, quickly rising from the table.

Seth sent Charling an urgent note stating it was imperative that Charling call on him immediately. His success hung on the fact that he must get the vowels before Charling approached Cecil Blakewell.

There was little chance of Seth failing in this purpose, for Lord Charling was aroused from a deep sleep at what he considered an ungodly hour in the morning. His valet stood trembling as he handed his master the urgent summons, sure of a sound reprimand. A bribe had prompted the valet's bold action.

Charling's bleary eyes focused on Mr. Blakewell's hasty note demanding his immediate attendance. The letter indicated it was of the utmost importance concerning the docks, and that he awaited, this very moment, Charling's call.

Lord Charling swore softly and threw back the covers while issuing orders to his valet to make haste. His head pounded with each movement. His tongue was thick in a mouth of cotton, which could be attributed to the brandy consumed in private celebration of his gambling coup. His hands shook slightly as he prepared to dress. Black coffee did not help.

Damn, he thought, why does Blakewell wish to see me at this moment? What could possibly be so important as to rouse a gentleman at practically the crack of dawn? A slight exaggeration, of course, but he had intended to collect the money from Cecil or the old earl, if possible, before seeing the American. Since he did not have the money in hand, he'd have to imply he was getting the investment money soon. He tucked the vowels in his jacket with the idea of seeing Cecil or the earl after his interview with Seth.

Charling looked in the mirror: his dissipated face stared back, and he shuddered. My luck has changed, he thought, and so shall my life. Placing his beaver hat upon his head, he set out to call upon Mr. Blakewell.

Angus offered Charling a hearty greeting upon his entrance and bade him be seated. Despite his careful grooming, the viscount's dissipation was obvious. Seth gave a perfunctory nod and murmured his cold greeting with barely concealed annoyance. Angus shot Seth a warning that was well taken. Seth hastily schooled his expression to one of detachment.

"I am informed you had a most successful night. You must be gratified, for now you will be able to join us as a partner. The profit, I promise you, could well provide your needs, or at least more modest needs for life, but I advise you to give up gambling. Luck is capricious and has a way of disappearing as quickly as it comes," Seth said while leaning against the mantel and barely disguising his disdain.

Charling was somewhat surprised. "News travels faster than I thought. How did you find out? I had hoped to collect the money before we met."

" 'Tis the kind of thing everyone hears as soon as it happens. Surely you haven't forgotten Mr. Grey's attendance last evening? Too intent on the game, perhaps? Well, no matter. I should like to relieve you of the vowels as payment for the venture, if that is agreeable. I shall have the papers drawn up today. You have been most kind to us since our arrival in England, and it pleases me to have you as a partner," Seth said, crossing the room and extending his hand to seal the bargain.

Angus watched the play acted out before him, and shook his head. *I must remember to tell Seth I hope always to remain in his good graces.*

Lord Charling smiled. It was true, he thought, without his patronage to meet the proper people, the Americans would never have had an opportunity to advance themselves so advantageously. He smirked in a self-satisfied manner. His circumstances did seem to have taken a turn to a brighter prospect.

"Why would you be willing to take the vowels?" Charling asked.

"That is of no concern to you, and as I have previously mentioned, you've been most helpful," Seth replied.

Lord Charling eyed him with suspicion. Well, what did he care as long as he got the funds to invest?

"I shall need some of the money for my expenses. Would an investment of nine thousand be sufficient and one thousand for my needs be agreeable?" he asked, hating the implications. He perceived his lofty class above these common venturers, and it was demeaning to appear groveling. It went against his blood. The necessity of doing so did not endear the Americans to him, in fact, he perceived a decided dislike. Ah, but needs must be met, he thought, and dismissed the feeling as beneath him.

"Certainly, it would mean only a smaller share, but that should not hamper the profits we're sure to reap. You do realize it will take time to build the docks. I expect to reap profits within a two-year period," Seth explained.

Charling frowned. He knew that was reasonable, but he would still be pressed for funds during that period. He shifted in his chair; the glories of having funds seemed to be once more beyond his immediate reach. Knowing the venture to be sound, he nodded in agreement. Scraping along was nothing new; he would do so again until the docks showed a profit. Haughtily handing over the gaming vowels as if he were giving a dog a bone, Charling prepared to leave.

Seth smiled menacingly as he took them without further comment.

They parted shortly after this conversation, and Seth fingered the written vowels Anthony had scribbled. The foolish young man, he thought. What a waste of a young life. Anthony needed a different direction.

The sobering thought of Miss Marshall under the care of such a weakling stabbed Seth's heart. Was there still time and would he be able to win her? He doubted it; by the time he was through, she would hate him.

Lord Cecil Blakewell was furious when he heard the news. He struck Anthony a blow along the side of his head in the rage he vented on his son.

"Prepare to leave at once. You are far to irresponsible to be allowed to remain in London. We leave for Chathram Manor this afternoon," Cecil bellowed.

Anthony was horrified at his stupidity and meekly prepared to return to Chathram Manor. He feared the encounter with his grandfather, whom he greatly admired. Anthony was still dazed at the ease in which he had been taken at play. It was almost as if the ivories were somehow crooked.

Cecil knew he would have to approach his father about covering the huge sum. A gentleman's honor compelled payment of any such debts. Considering the problems gaming had caused in his life, and weighed it so heavily, he sat in sullen silence all the way to Surrey. Anthony was grateful for the reprieve.

Seth called on Quentin Marshall on the pretense of business but in greater hopes of seeing Miss Marshall. He was welcomed by the squire, who now had the promissory note and was excited to learn the project was about to get under way.

When they had finished with their business, Seth tucked the note in his inside pocket and asked if Squire Marshall might allow him to escort Miss Marshall for an outing.

"Perhaps, she would enjoy a carriage ride," Seth said, hoping against hope she would accept.

Marshall cast him a knowing glance but made no reference to Anthony, and Seth wondered if he had heard the gossip. The news had not yet reached Marshall's ears.

Not surprising, the squire agreed. If his daughter did not have a previous engagement, a ride would be acceptable to him.

Caroline and Sissy were sitting with Annemarie when Quentin entered the morning room.

"Mr. Blakewell is here and wishes to invite Annemarie to join him for a ride in the park," he said, expecting the disapproving look he received from his wife.

Caroline slowly lowered her needle and scowled. "Good heavens, that man! Whatever for? She's to be engaged to Lord Anthony. I do not think it advisable."

Anne's heart gave a little tumble. She had missed seeing

him. In fact, she had looked for him at every entertainment they had attended, until she learned he had been gone from London for several days.

"Mother, I should like to take an outing. He is pleasant and I see no harm in accompanying him," Anne said, beginning to rise.

"Caroline, I think it would be rude to refuse. I am interested in his friendship. It can do no harm for her to be seen with him riding in an open carriage in the park," Quentin answered. "Besides, the betrothal has not been announced."

"She's young, Caroline, and must be bored to tears sitting while we do needlepoint. It's hardly her idea of a morning's diversion. Go, enjoy yourself," Sissy gently commanded.

Caroline was affronted at the usurping of her wishes, but she remained silent rather than make an issue. She frowned; Blakewell was far too attractive, and she knew all too well where that could lead.

Annemarie left the room before her mother changed her mind, breathlessly calling to Flora, "Do hurry! Mr. Blakewell has invited me for a carriage ride."

Flora happily assisted her mistress into a warm green velvet pelisse with fur *mancherons*, collar, and cuffs. The matching shallow-crowned bonnet with its deep brim sported feathers and looped ribbons. Her brown kid gloves matched the pointed slippers that tied with ribbons. Anne was a picture of a very fashionable young lady, and she smiled with approval. Flora was as pleased as a mother hen, and her eyes shone with interested speculation at her mistress's obvious excitement.

Mr. Blakewell's response was even more appreciative as she descended the steps and greeted him. He extended his hand and gazed into her eyes.

"Ah, a pleasure to see you once more, Miss Marshall.

The day is brisk, but the sun promises a little warmth and it should be a perfect outing,'' he said.

She smiled up to him and a telling flush glowed on her cheeks. Her tilted eyes sparkled with excitement, and Seth's heart raced at the sight of her. He realized how much he had longed to see her.

He assisted her into the carriage and took his seat, beaming all the while with the pleasure of being with her. The pleasure was mutual, and the atmosphere between them crackled with excitement and buoyant good humor.

Red and golden leaves still clung to the trees, while others fluttered down with the soft breeze, covering the ground with a golden carpet. The park was glorious and reminded Anne of her ride with Anthony the day he had proposed. The excitement of being next to Mr. Blakewell drew a comparison that made her feelings toward Anthony seem sadly dull.

Anne caught her breath. "It's so beautiful! It's almost enough to change my mind about London."

"How so? You're not fond of London?" he asked.

"I find far more pleasure in the country with my horses. That is one reason I'm so delighted to be going down to Surrey for the hunt party at Chathram Manor."

"I shall be joining that party and look forward to it. Your 'country' is a most civilized place compared to the countryside of my home. Still, somehow I can picture you there. You would love it, I know," he said.

"How can you be sure? The frontier might just be too isolated for me," she teased.

"I have a feeling it is the horses you like better than people. Am I correct?"

Annemarie glanced over to him. His strong profile was certainly handsome. There was an exotic quality about him that was very compelling. He turned to look at her, leveling his smoky gray-green eyes on hers.

"It's not people that I dislike, only pretension," she softly said.

He smiled and nodded in approval. "And so I thought."

"You have seen me no more than a few times. How can you presume to know any more than the slightest information about me?" she said dryly.

Seth chuckled. "I first saw you astride a magnificent horse with your sherry hair flying in the wind. I know more than you suppose, and at the risk of sounding too bold I like very much what I have seen and know."

Anne fell silent. They had entered dangerous territory. She was tempted to say she liked what she saw and knew about him, but of course, she did not. They rode a little while without speaking.

Seth suddenly turned to her. "Have I offended you? You do not strike me as one who would be so offended by my frankness," he said.

"You did not offend me. I am to be betrothed to Lord Anthony Blakewell and think it best you not speak in such a manner."

Seth did not immediately reply. He had started down a path that was certain to bring her hatred, not her love. How foolish he was to still seek her out. She was a striking, capable woman, and he could not accept her belonging to anyone else. She belonged by his side, taming his growing empire and raising a houseful of sons. What strapping sons they would make! A flame lit his eyes.

His expression caused a delicious shiver to travel her body. She blushed. Seth smiled disarmingly, knowing that an affinity existed between them, for she had felt his emotion almost as soon as he did.

He directed the horses off the well-traveled road along a narrow rutted path. The branches of the trees brushed them both, even knocking Anne's bonnet askew. Anne knew she should protest, but she did not. To speak would break a spell that surrounded them, and for now she had no wish to do that.

Seth halted the horses. He turned to her. He reached out and touched her cheek.

Annemarie sat still, her pulse pounding. "I think we ought to . . ."

Her words faded in the soft air as his face moved closer. He circled her waist with his strong arms and pulled her easily to him. No protest was uttered as his mouth covered hers with a soft, tender kiss. He kissed her again, and with more passion. Her arms went around his neck.

"Anne," he whispered, "you belong to me. You are everything I could want," he whispered soft, caressing words. Her yielding, warm, womanly body brought trembling desire pulsing through him.

Anne rested her head on his broad chest. She could hear the swift pounding of his heart. She trembled. Her head swam with swirling emotions. He drew her even tighter to his powerful body, and she, who had never felt the need to belong to a man, found a safe haven in his arms.

He placed his fingers on her chin and raised her face once more to his. He studied the gold-flecked eyes, so entrancing with their thick black lashes. His gaze traveled to her full, warm mouth, and he kissed her again; this time his passion brought him to probe the soft sweetness of her mouth. A soft groan escaped his lips as he placed his cheek against hers. "Anne, I cannot let you go. Say you will be mine."

Be his, Anne thought. It would never be permitted. She raised her hands to his chest and gently pushed him away. She looked up into his splendid eyes, now aflame with desire. Oh, how wrong of me to encourage this!

"I have done you a disservice. I should not have allowed

you to kiss me. I am to marry Anthony. It is settled with our families," she said, tears springing to her eyes.

"Call it fate, whatever. You belong in my arms. It did not displease you," he said.

"No, it pleased me. I never knew a kiss could make me feel so alive. I wanted you to kiss me. Nevertheless, it is my fault. I am to wed Lord Anthony and it was wrong of me to wish your attentions. Forgive me."

Seth laughed.

Anne's eyes widened. "What amuses you so? I don't find it funny . . . not in the slightest!" she said angrily.

"Miss Marshall, most young ladies would be berating me for taking such liberties, and you apologize. I am amazed. You are unique. All the more reason to claim you."

"Well, obviously you are more knowledgeable of what young ladies do in this situation. You obviously have had more experience in this vein of endeavor, which makes me realize I have all the reason to *not* belong to you. Take me home."

Seth chuckled, then spent the longest time maneuvering the horses and carriage back out of the narrow path.

When at last he had managed to get the carriage out onto main road, he turned to her. "You see it is easier to get into a situation, but far more difficult to extricate oneself. I fear it will be so with us," he said, flicking the reins to set the horses into motion.

Returning her to the Suttons' town house, he reached over and removed a leaf of pure gold from her bonnet and handed it to her. "In remembrance of our outing. Keep in mind what I said."

Miss Annemarie Marshall spent the entire night remembering his kiss, the comfort of his arms . . . in fact, everything he did and said.

13

Guests began arriving for the Chathram hunt, sending the servants into a pitch of activity. It was traditionally a large party, for few refused the opportunity to attend. Carriages arrived piled high with voluminous quantities of baggage holding everything that the visitors deemed necessary to properly impress other guests. Many were to stay for several days and brought their personal servants and mounts.

Pandemonium reigned in the stables, while each groom settled his master's horse. They vied for status by extolling the superior merits of each animal in their charge.

A game of dice was enthusiastically played behind the stored hay, well out of sight. The laughter and curses concerning the game added to the noise and apparently went unnoticed, for none interfered.

Since Chathram Manor had no mistress, the duties fell to the housekeeper, Mrs. Hartley, who had successfully executed the meals and ball for years.

The household was in equal turmoil with every lady's maid and valet executing the needs of what, they assured one another, were impossible tasks, dictated by the most exacting employers in all the realm. Each servant, nodding with sympathy, allowed to the others that their employers were the most demanding, and it was a good thing the master had the likes of themselves to carry on.

The entry hall rang with greetings, laughter, and flirtatious glances that promised much. The back stairs were no less busy with hot water being carried up and used water down. A tray of sherry and biscuits or a ruff freshly pressed, since becoming impossibly crushed in a trunk, was whisked off efficiently to waiting *beau monde*. An air of excitement hung over both stairways, but the quiet sense of hidden resignation hovered only among those in the back hall.

Anthony had been home for ten days under disgrace. Chathram was furious and refused outright to consider his betrothal to Annemarie, stating she didn't need such a fool for a husband.

The old earl had written Addison asking to retrieve the debts from Lord Charling and was amazed to find that Mr. Blakewell had assumed those debts. He awaited the arrival of the strange young man in order to question him as to exactly why he had taken the vowels, attributing all manner of devious motives to such an act.

Arriving in the midafternoon, Seth and Angus handed the footman their greatcoats and hats only to be told that the Earl of Chathram wished to see Seth immediately upon his entrance.

Not surprised by the request, Seth sauntered into the same library in which they had previously spoken. Since Seth rarely sauntered anywhere, it indicated his reluctant expectation of the reason for this demand.

The dignified earl briskly motioned Seth to be seated. Coming directly to the point, he said, "It has come to my attention that you have purchased all Anthony's gaming vowels. Why?"

Seth was taken completely by surprise. Of course, Addison has informed me. I should have thought of that.

"I bought them to have a bargaining power over the family that betrayed my father," he honestly replied.

"To acquire ill-gotten gains? Or recognition as heir?" This elderly gentleman angrily spat his words, for this honesty had not been expected.

"Neither. I sought justified revenge."

"When is revenge ever justified?" Chathram asked. "It is written that vengeance is the Lord's."

"I came to meet the relations and to clear my father's name. I have not been allowed that privilege. First, I was refused admittance, then refused recognition of my claim. I now have the power to extract that recognition for my father," Seth said, speaking with the satisfaction of his position.

"Indeed? Do you? I think not. A blackguard does not demand what I cannot in all honesty give in agreement. Having in your possession items belonging to John does not prove you are his son. You could be any self-seeking adventurer."

A derisive smile appeared on the aquiline face of the American. "Then I shall tell you the whole story. I had hoped not to, thinking it unnecessary, but you will hear the sordid details. Doubt still lingers, and you will not be satisfied until you do, but you will be infinitely more saddened when you have."

"I am not compelled to listen," Chathram challenged.

"Then you will always wonder if, by chance, I am who I say I am. Perhaps that is of no import, I cannot say. If I judge this family by its previous actions, then you will not wish to know the truth. It is not a pleasant story, I assure you," Seth said, leaning back in his chair. His hand swept the air as if to dismiss the tale, left untold. The easy movement of his body belied the sharp-witted glint of his eyes. He watched his grandfather intently a moment, then continued.

"Cecil is certainly not fit to be the next earl. Look to Anthony and you see a young man that needs discipline and purpose to his life. I'd like to take Anthony back to Georgia for a year or two and let him work as he's never worked before. A little sweat and muscle might make a man of him. The house of Chathram is in desperate need of a worthy man to carry on the line, not an attempted murderer or a weak popinjay," Seth said. He was as angry as the earl now. His voice had risen in a strong, clipped pace.

Chathram sat back, appalled by the harsh words. "Tell me your story," he commanded.

Seth proceeded to do so, leaving no detail out. He was a free American, an independent man, not an interloper or adventurer.

A silence followed the end of his tale.

"I think I have suspected this. Somehow I have read it in Cecil's eyes without recognizing it. One can refuse to accept what is plain to see but too painful to contemplate. What do you want from me?" Chathram asked, completely drained of any hauteur. His hands shook and an ashen color lingered around his mouth.

"I do not wish to claim my inheritance. I will return to America as soon as possible. You might consider my taking Anthony with me for a time. Trust me, he'll come back a man, not the foolish wastrel that he now is becoming. However, I know he is to wed Miss Marshall, and that will be disastrous for her . . . and me."

"He is not to marry Miss Marshall. I have refused permission. I have not told the squire, but I intend to do so this weekend. It is obvious Quentin Marshall has used his knowledge in this matter to his advantage. My instincts did not fail me in this matter, although my refusal was for other reasons. I am too fond of Miss Marshall to saddle her with the likes of Anthony. But what is it to you?'' he asked.

''The minute I saw her, I knew she belonged to me. She was meant for the freedom of the new land without the ridiculous restrictions of society. She is all that I desire. Believe me, I had not thought to fall in love. It has complicated my plans totally.''

A hearty laugh escaped the earl. ''Indeed, I can understand why. You can hardly take revenge and win the lady's hand. So the proud American succumbs to the charms of an English maid. I think providence has had a bit of revenge on you, my lad.''

''You may find it amusing, but I am at my wit's end. I need her,'' Seth said, pleased that some humor had been restored. He regretted his anger and the telling of the story in such blatant details.

''Then woo her. Win her. You seem a bold-enough fellow—certainly by your actions one might judge you so. I shall watch all this unfold with relish. You have the weekend. Let us watch what my bold American grandson can manage.''

Seth smiled at the word *grandson,* and his heart lifted at the prospect of the challenge. He felt Miss Marshall was not indifferent to him.

''I am part Indian and will return to America. Those are also drawbacks to my suit. I can manage the squire, but Miss Marshall will not be so compliant, I'm sure.''

''I should hope not. She would not be worthy of you if she were. If you think being part Indian would make a difference to Annemarie, you do not know her at all. Actually gives you a bit of dash, to my way of thinking. Ladies are surely not immune to your fine appearance, and you're man enough to seek what you wish. Nothing has apparently stopped you before,'' Chathram said.

Seth considered his words and smiled. ''Then we are agreed; this conversation goes no further. John was your son and loved you. That is the mission for which I came.''

''I accept your story as the truth. We will let it rest. I am pleased with the news, for I loved John dearly. Cecil has paid for his deed many times over, I assure you. He has been but a shadow of himself since that night. I will reimburse you for the gambling debts. Keep the vowels as an excuse for taking Anthony with you. Make him work like the devil and send him back to be a worthy Earl of Chathram, one that we can be proud of,'' he said, rising slowly.

''Thank you, sir. I'll see what I can manage with the enchanting Miss Marshall.''

''Enchanting, is it? Gad, man you're besotted.'' The earl chuckled.

''So I've been told,'' Seth answered dryly, but his eyes twinkled.

They parted company. Seth was saddened by the weary slump of the elderly gentleman. He was too old to hear such information, yet he had accepted it as though he had truly known it. Seth shrugged with regret, pain clearly marking his eyes. He left to seek Angus in hopes of a few understanding words from his friend. This whole venture was certainly not the simple task he had expected.

Miss Marshall had arrived at Sutton Hall later in the day. Squire Marshall and his family would not be staying at Chathram Manor because Sutton Hall was in close proximity. They would, of course, be attending all the social events.

Anne lost no time changing into a riding habit and entering

the stables. Calling a hearty greeting to McGuire, she walked directly to Taliesin's stall.

"Let's take my fine hunter for a ride," she cooed.

"He's anxious for a run," McGuire agreed.

"Not as much as I," she said with a lilting laugh.

Mounted on the back of the huge animal, she set off at a swift pace. Taliesin was as delighted as his mistress.

The sun was dropping along the hills, sending late, golden light and darkening shadows along the vales. Anne knew she must return home in order to prepare for the evening's dinner at Chathram. She frowned a little. The announcement of her engagement would be made at the ball, and the thought caused a sigh to escape her lips.

The late-afternoon sun sent an illusion of warmth throughout the countryside, but the air was growing chilly. Just as she pulled on the reins, she heard the sound of an approaching horse.

She watched the tall, dark American riding toward her, and she waited with a slight catch in her breath and a quickening of her pulse.

He rode well, with an easy manner that somehow set him apart from the English gentlemen. A subtle distinction, to be sure, and not one to be noticed by many, she mused. The surety with which he rode indicated a basic harmony with the horse as a partner. She did not think he would ever choose a horse merely to display himself advantageously. Anne shook her head at her fanciful thoughts as Seth Blakewell approached her side.

" 'Evening, ma'am. What a stroke of luck! Imagine my finding you here," he said, feigning surprise. A twinkle gleamed in his eyes. He knew she would ride at her first opportunity and had waited in hopes of finding her.

"Indeed, a mere coincidence, I'm sure," Anne replied dryly, but her smile gave away her true response.

"Hm, wonderful time of day to be riding. I thought I'd find you out," he said, pulling in his reins as he maneuvered next to her.

Taliesin tossed his head and shied slightly. He felt the tension in his mistress at the approaching gentleman.

"Yes, it is wonderful riding without hampering crowds. This is where I belong."

"May I ride a way with you?" Seth asked.

"I'm about to return, but you may accompany me if you wish," she replied, watching his tanned face glow with late-afternoon sunshine.

"You will be attending the dinner held at Chathram Manor tonight?" Seth asked.

"Yes, I shall be at most of the events. You may offer me your best wishes. The announcement of my betrothal to Lord Anthony will be made at the hunt ball." She eagerly imparted this information. She watched his face for a sign of expression. None was forthcoming. This annoyed her, somehow.

"If that is what will make you happy, I can do nothing but wish you well. I somehow believe neither fact will prove to be the case. But, no matter, you have my felicitations," he said, turning his face from hers. He could not be the one to tell her there would be no betrothal.

Anne knew she should let the remark go by. In fact, she allowed a few seconds to pass as she considered his remark. "Of course it is what I wish, or I would not do so," she said.

"Is that why you allowed me to kiss you?" he asked.

Anne flushed. "You are too unkind to remind me of that indiscretion." She flicked her reins to urge the horse forward.

Seth increased his speed to catch her. He reached for her

reins and slowed her pace. "Forgive me, I was wrong to bring up the subject. It is one, unfortunately, that has not left my mind for any length of time," he said, watching her.

"You are forgiven. Please do not mention it again. I am to wed another," she tersely replied.

"Can I approach the subject if you don't wed another?" he teased.

Anne smiled. "You are mistaken, sir; I will wed Lord Anthony, as promised."

"It's not announced yet. Marry me instead. Come to America. In all honesty, it is where you belong. At my side, of course," he urged.

The afternoon shadows heightened the planes of his face, making his exotic features even more compelling. He looked as tempting as Lucifer.

Anne raised her chin. "I don't believe what I'm hearing! How can you offer for me? You don't even know me. I have no dowry and am promised to someone else. Are all Americans so impulsive?"

"It is my one chance . . . to propose before it is announced. We'd suit. I knew the moment I saw you. I don't need a dowry. Americans believe a gentleman makes his own money," he said.

"You mean no man makes advantageous marriages? They all marry for love?" she taunted.

Seth laughed. "You have me. Many marriages are made for expediency. Mine shall not. So, Miss Marshall, marry me. Come be my love, as poets say, but put as a purely American plea, stand by my side and help tame a frontier," he said with a serious tremor in his voice. His eyes glowed like smoky jade. He edged his horse closer and reached out his hand.

Annemarie was totally hypnotized by his smoldering eyes. She was again falling under the spell of his considerable charm. She watched his hand reach for her and a tingle ran the length of her back. She spurred her horse forward in panic.

"Good afternoon, Mr. Blakewell," she called over her shoulder.

"Marry me, ma'am," he called after her and softly laughed as she turned to look at him. He saluted her smartly, and Anne could not help but smile.

"Absolutely not," she called back, and increased the distance between them as if her life depended on it. Perhaps it did.

Seth watched her ride away. What an enchanting woman! She'll be mine, Seth vowed, even if he had to kidnap her. The idea appealed to him and he softly chuckled. He shrugged his shoulders and thought, Whatever it takes, she's mine.

During dinner they were seated some distance from each other. Anne thought this a blessing when she took her place on the opposite side of the long walnut table. The distance, however, was only physical. She was conscious of him every minute. Often she found his eyes resting on her. She could feel his gaze when trying desperately not to look his way.

Seth observed Anne gaily talking to her dinner partners and became annoyed that she seemed to ignore him. She looked his way several times, but turned immediately to one of her partners—one being Lord Anthony.

He watched them together and realized for certain they were bound solely by friendship. Lord Anthony was no man in love, he observed by noting the young man's casual attitude toward Miss Marshall. Seth was pleased with this observation and would have been happier had he known how much his presence was affecting her.

When the gentlemen joined the ladies after their port, Seth approached Anne. She stood next to Lord Anthony and several other guests. He could do no more than exchange a few pleasantries. Seth stood more as an observer than a participant. English drawing-room banter left him nonplussed. It was foreign to his experience.

Slightly bored, he glanced around the room and saw Angus standing with Miss Markham. Seth smiled at the sight of the handsome redhead charming the wide-eyed Miss Markham. Angus seems to be faring rather well, he thought, far better than I. Seth glanced back to Miss Marshall. His somber thoughts showed as a sullen expression on his finely chiseled face.

When the gathered guests were about to be presented with the dubious pleasure of hearing Lady Dennington sing, Seth glowered. Why in the hell am I here? he chastised himself. Should I seek a lady who won't even look at me, he thought with a wry smile?

"My, that's the first smile I've seen all evening."

Seth turned to find Annemarie standing next to him. He flushed.

"How do you bear such insipid conversations?" he asked.

Anne laughed. "I'll tell you a secret. I hate them."

Seth looked into her hazel eyes and suddenly the night had promise.

"I'm surprised you noticed," he said.

"Noticed what?"

"That I hadn't smiled. It pleases me to know you're interested enough to remark upon it."

Anne clenched her hands and a flicker of annoyance sparked in her eyes. "You are the most insufferable man I've ever met! To note glowering scowls hardly denotes interest. Quite the contrary, it allows one to learn how very bad-tempered you are."

"Bad-tempered? I'm a lamb. I hoped all evening to speak with you, but now I've only managed to anger you. I'm not insufferable, only clumsy. Could we begin again? My, Miss Marshall, you are a picture of all that is lovely. I stand in awe at the sight of you,'' he said, and offered a slight bow.

Anne smiled. ''Why, you can offer the same hollow compliments with the best of them.''

''Ah, there you are wrong. The pretty speech was actually parroted from some drawing-room dandy, but the sentiments are my own.''

Anne and Seth stood looking at each other for a moment.

''I must speak with someone, excuse me please,'' Anne said as she started to move away.

''Running away again?'' Seth asked.

''Yes. With you I always end up in a situation from which I feel I might not escape,'' she hissed.

''At last, I'm getting somewhere,'' he said.

14

The crisp, invigorating air heightened the excitement among the riders gathering in the Chathram courtyard. Laughter mingled with bantering as eager participants of the hunt challenged one another on the possible outcome.

Anne, seated on her magnificent black stallion, reflected the same anticipation with the radiance of her glowing eyes and rosy cheeks. She wore a black serge habit. The neck sported a pristine ruff, a white feather curled along her hat, and black boots peeked out from the hem of her skirt. She was always at home on horseback, and her confidence showed in each movement.

Admiration was expressed on the fine points of her sleek Irish hunter by several gentlemen whose interest might be directed to either rider or horse.

"A bit much to handle, for a lady, I should think," Lord Ripton remarked.

"He suits me well. He's the finest hunter I've ever owned," Anne replied.

"An Irish hunter has its place, but I'll take the English Thoroughbred any day," he boasted, smartly maneuvering his superior stallion for the approval of the other riders.

Lady Edwell, who considered herself an excellent equestrian and cared little for any who might usurp her standing or center of attention, smiled toward Lady Ashton.

"She's suited to an Irish hunter," she remarked with a gleam of malice.

Lady Ashton, looking dainty seated carefully on a smaller, gentler horse, raised a delicate eyebrow. "I find I am all admiration for her handsome appearance."

"Great heavens!" Lady Edwell laughed. "You are far too ladylike for such a mighty horse. Most women would be. It takes an Amazon to handle such a brute."

The remark filtered back to Anne. They pass all bearing— I'll outride the lot of them, she thought defiantly. She maneuvered the horse away from the gossips with a military bearing and effortless ease. Her show of bravado was childish, and she knew it.

Anthony's arrival distracted her annoyance when she noted his scowling face, petulant set of mouth, and worried eyes. He managed a wan smile when he saw her. "Good morning, Anne. You look magnificent. I see you're cutting quite a dash. One can always tell one's success by how soon the tabbies unsheathe their claws," he teased. "Believe me, you'll soon show the riding skill few of them possess. I'll ride by your side, if I'm able to keep up with you."

"Good morning, Anthony. You always manage to put things right. But you do not look as though your heart is in this day's chase. What is wrong?"

"Anne, I must speak with you later. It is of the utmost importance. I'm sorry," he said softly.

"Whatever for?" she asked, aware of the agitation underlying his hesitant manner.

"We'll speak later. Just be careful you don't overrun the quarry with that beast," he teased, trying to offer a lighter tone.

"How infamous of you to suggest such a thing," she said, then laughed.

Mr. Seth Blakewell, looking absolutely splendid in his dark

coat and beige breeches, entered the courtyard. The hardened frontiersman cut a dash that set him apart in the most compelling way. His ruggedness attracted the attention of most ladies present. It was simply unmasked, male animal magnetism seldom seen among the English gentry. The hint of luxury or indulgent living had no place in his countenance.

Annemarie noticed him immediately and thought him by far the most outstanding man present. She smiled at him and matched his interested gaze. A little tremor ran through her body. Unlike her usual, direct manner, she blushed and lowered her eyes. She turned her head away and looked, unseeing, toward the other guests.

Seth brought his horse to her other side. "You'd not find a finer morning for such an event," he said as he nodded recognition to Anthony. Anthony's frown deepened. A small smile played on the American's lips. "Are you not for the morning's ride to hounds, Lord Anthony?" he asked.

Anthony scrutinized the tall gentleman and felt an uneasy sense of the man's power, almost as if he held some secret over him. It was disconcerting because the feeling was intense and unexpected, and he could not understand the reason for it.

"Indeed, I am. I like nothing better. Shall we move out, Anne? The hunt master is about to begin the chase," he said, moving his horse forward.

Anne glanced at Seth, who nodded slightly with an absolutely infuriating confidence. Silently he seemed to say, I know all that you hide in your heart. She turned sharply away and followed Anthony's lead. The man was impertinent. She had only herself to blame. He made too much of a kiss. She would let him know that fact, in no uncertain terms.

The hunt began with the barking hounds suddenly released into a frenzy of pursuit.

The morning was glorious, with the sun streaming through

the filtering leaves in a world all gold and red. Anne's spirits soared as she smoothly cleared the first jump. Anthony rode not far from her right, and she caught his look of approval.

The riders began to scatter as the faster horses and the more aggressive riders pressed forward. Because of the hours spent in a saddle, Seth was obviously the best horseman in the group. He was accustomed to traveling rough terrain for long periods of time. When he entered a narrow path through a small wooded area into a glade, Anne was several lengths behind him, followed by Lord Anthony. The hooves pounded the hard ground, echoing throughout the forest. Seth lowered his head to avoid a low-hanging branch just as he entered the opposite side of the woods. A shot rang out.

Seth heard the bullet pass over his head by inches. He lowered his body closer to the stallion when the second shot exploded into the horse beneath him. The gallant horse stumbled and fell, taking Seth with him. He was pinned to the ground by the deadweight of the huge animal. He was momentarily stunned, and it took him a moment to realize what had happened.

Annemarie saw the accident and cried out. When she reached the fallen horse and rider, she struggled as she tried to dismount, hampered by her skirt. Finally free, she slid to the ground and rushed to the downed horse and rider.

Lord Anthony reached their side just as Anne knelt beside Mr. Blakewell. Taliesin, sensing danger, reared. Anne rose to grapple with its bridle to bring the mighty stallion under control.

"Anthony, head off the riders," she cried, still holding the bridle and realizing they were in danger from the thundering, oncoming horses. Anne tethered Taliesin and turned to aid Seth.

Laboring to extricate himself, Seth was in pain and uncertain whether his leg was broken.

"Let me help," Anne cried, but the deadweight of the horse was more than her strength could manage. She sat back on her knees at a loss for what to do next.

Anthony warned the riders to turn aside and returned as soon as possible to their aid, and together they managed to free Blakewell.

Seth sat a moment collecting his wits. Gingerly moving his booted leg, he ascertained it was not broken. It felt bruised and sore. Suddenly his attention shifted and his eyes narrowed as he scanned the woods. He rose carefully, first trying his leg, then he began searching the undergrowth with keen eyes. Slowly entering the brush at the side of the path, he observed broken branches and matted grass where the assailant had apparently lain in ambush.

He winced with pain as he dropped to one knee. Viewing the path and the angle, he could see the attacker had had an easy shot. So easy, in fact, it appeared to be only a warning. But why in the hell kill an animal? Seth swore. He ran his hand along the grass where small plants were bent and matted, indicating exactly the spot on which the assailant had waited. Seth noted some blades of grass slowly returning to an upright position. The perpetrator had obviously quit the scene just seconds after the firing of the weapon. Seth tried to recall any sounds he had heard, but the cries of their party had blocked out any such memory.

As he continued to run his hand along the grass, a glitter of metal among dry leaves caught his eye. He reached down and picked up a fine gold button, slowly examined the exquisite quality, and slipped it into his pocket.

"I reckon our assailant has quit the scene," he said mildly, knowing the chance to overtake him had slipped away.

"We are safe enough now," Seth said.

Anne and Anthony still stood on the path staring through the brush at Seth.

"Oh, surely it was just a poacher," Anne exclaimed. "Who would wish to harm you?"

"Who, indeed?" Seth replied derisively as he continued searching the area. The shot had come from ground level, not from a sniper hidden in the branches of a tree. He absently rubbed his sore and bruised leg as he made his way through the brush and back onto the path.

Dropping to the side of his prone horse, he ran his hand over the smooth hair of the beautiful animal. Seth cursed the man who would perpetrate such a vile crime. He knew the bullet had been meant for him, to either kill or frighten him, and a seething anger flashed fire in his eyes. His jaw tightened and a hardness appeared upon his face that spoke nothing but hatred.

Anne gasped at his fierce look. "It had to be an accident. No one would deliberately try to shoot you," she uttered in disbelieving shock.

He turned to rest his uncomfortably penetrating eyes on her, but did not reply. Reaching for Taliesin's reins, he commanded Anne to mount. Settling her in the saddle, he removed her foot from the stirrup, placing his own in it. He winced with pain as he swung up behind her sidesaddle. The animal was large, but there was precious little room behind the saddle. Taliesin began to reject the added and unusual weight.

"Be still, Taliesin, we need you to behave," Anne implored. The black stallion heard the pleading voice of its mistress and accepted the added burden.

Seth placed his arms around Annemarie and took the reins. He could feel her body trembling with fright.

Seth turned to Lord Anthony. "Get help for the horse, although it is too late. We will return to the hall. There are some questions to be asked . . . and answered.

"The assailant is only minutes ahead of us. It is my guess he has rejoined the rest of the riders so as not to be noticed. We will wait for their return," he said, his lips uncomfortably close to her cheek.

"How do you know?" Anne asked.

"The grass was still returning to an upright position. He had a perfect opportunity to kill me. It is my thought I am being warned."

"How can you come to so many conclusions? It was merely a poacher. And how can you be so sure that was where he was hiding?"

"Miss Marshall, I spent many summers of my youth with my grandmother's people. I've learned tracking and survival, skills few Englishmen know," Seth said, deliberately leaning closer to her.

She could feel the strength and warmth of his strong body and arms. "Your mother's people? Who are your mother's people?"

"Why, Miss Marshall, I'm part Creek Indian, didn't you know?" he asked with a low resonance to his voice. He knew very well the information was new to her and wished he could see her face.

"No . . . I did not. That must be very interesting," she feebly replied. What an inane remark, she thought. An Indian, imagine! Perhaps that was what made him so unusually attractive and, well, mysterious. And she smiled as she turned her head to try to look at him.

Seth tightened his arms about her. "How does it feel to be surrounded by an Indian? Your mother says she would faint at such a frightful experience." He laughed softly.

Anne could feel his breath on her cheek and thought, If I faint, it will be from your disconcerting nearness. This thought amused her and she returned the laugh, but not for the same reason.

Seth leaned his face closer and placed a light kiss on her cheek.

"Mr. Blakewell, you may have me surrounded, but are you using fair methods for surrender?"

This time Seth laughed joyously. "Ma'am, it is my experience that this method is used universally. And to success, if one is to judge by the growing population."

Anne felt a rush of embarrassment. "You place too much value on your charm, Mr. Blakewell. I may be surrounded but not defeated."

"That's the spirit. I would have it no other way," he teased.

"Mr. Blakewell, you don't seem to understand. You don't have it . . . any way. I may be in your arms, only due to unfortunate circumstances. You could hardly call it willingly," she snapped.

"I find the experience delightful and will be nothing but bereft when I must release you," he continued, pressing the advantage of her nearness. "I'm tempted to continue riding and simply capture you and take you away."

"I can unseat you in a second by word command, I assure you," she hotly replied.

"Ah, and well I know it. Therefore, I shall refrain from further conversation that so obviously annoys you. However, you cannot keep me from the enjoyment of having my arms about you."

"You're far too bold," she tartly replied.

"And that you may attribute to the American blood I carry." He brushed his lips against her cheek.

"You simply refuse to accept that I am to wed Lord Anthony."

"Is it for love or the advantages as the wife of the future Earl of Chathram?" he crudely asked.

Annemarie squeezed her eyes tight to fight back threatening tears. His remark was not far from the mark, but it hurt neverthess.

Nothing more was said on the remaining ride to the Chathram stable yard. Despite all that had happened, she felt pleasure in the warmth and strength of his body. Upon entering the cobbled yard, they were met by the earl's anxious grooms, who had been told of the incident by Anthony. Seth deftly slipped off the horse. He stood and reached up, placing his hands around Anne's waist. Their eyes met a moment. He studied her expression as he gently lifted her down.

Anne was not unmoved, and it showed in her heightened color and the warmth of her eyes. His dangerous attraction made her too vulnerable, and she briskly released herself from his hold.

Seth stepped back and dropped his arms. "We'll continue our conversation at a more opportune moment," he said with a wicked twinkle in his eyes.

"You are mistaken, sir. I will guard against such a time," she said, and turned to the direction of the house.

Anne was shaken by the recent events, but it was this disconcerting man from whom she needed to escape. She scurried across the stone courtyard as if the hounds of hell were after her. She quickly entered Chathram Manor and made her way to the earl's library. Shutting the door, she leaned against it.

Mr. Blakewell was affecting her beyond all that was proper. Here she was, about to be betrothed, and allowing the handsome American to kiss her without any convincing protest. What was happening to her? She paced the floor in agitation. All sense seemed to escape her. Her thoughts tumbled in jumbled chaos, and she knew in only moments the events concerning the shooting would be the excited topic of conversation. She would have to answer questions for which she had no answer.

The sound of returning horses caught her attention, and she turned to cross the room and stand by the tall windows. The view allowed a complete survey of the well-trimmed maze planted when such devices were considered the very thing. She smiled a moment wondering how many kisses had been stolen in that maze under the unknown gazes of occupants from this room.

Anne watched Cecil Blakewell hurrying along the stone walk. Just as she was about to turn away, she saw Seth Blakewell quickly overtake him. The two men stood in animated conversation. It appeared to be an angry confrontation. Cecil backed up and turned to leave, Seth grabbed his arm and forced him into the walk of the maze. Cecil was offering a violent protest.

Seth removed an object from his pocket and grabbed Cecil's coat. Lord Blakewell brought up his arm in a blow to throw off Seth's hand. In response Mr. Blakewell delivered a facer that sent Cecil reeling. The American pursued the Englishman and proceeded to beat him with a series of blows that left Cecil on his knees with blood streaming from a fast-swelling nose.

Seth stood, feet apart, apparently continuing to offer a violent tirade. He reached down and picked up limp, dangling Cecil. Covering his face with his arms to ward off any further blows, Cecil stood trembling. Seth paused, turned on his heel, and strode from the maze.

Anne was horrified. What was the reason for this barbaric attack? The man was a savage!

As it happened, the Earl of Chathram was afforded the

same view from his quarters, which were directly over the library. The elderly gentleman stood transfixed by the appalling sight before his eyes. He was astounded by the attack and the swift defeat of the protesting Cecil. Was this a direct assault for Seth's grievance against Cecil?

The earl was given to understand in unspoken agreement that Blackwell had no desire or intention of harming Cecil. There was an explanation, and he would have it.

Damn, I've sired a lineage of idiots and I am forever doomed to sorting out their inadequacies, he thought.

The Earl of Chathram rang for his valet and requested the presence of Mr. Seth Blackwell immediately upon his return to the house.

15

Seth entered his grandfather's quarters to find the elderly gentleman standing beside the tall windows. The light streamed over his lined face, emphasizing his great age. His pale eyes were cool and appraising.

"Come here," Chathram commanded with an impatient gesture of his hand.

Crossing the room with a swift stride, Seth halted beside him. Their eyes locked a moment. Lord Blackwell turned his head to look out the window, and Seth's eyes followed. Below him stretched the vista of the back terrace and the boxwood maze. The labyrinth was in full view from the height of the room.

Instant understanding flickered in Seth's eyes. A ridiculous and superfluous thought occurred to him. How many kisses stolen in the fale sense of privacy had been viewed from the upper windows over the years? A small, ironic smile played upon his mouth for a second time.

The earl was affronted by Seth's look of amusement. "Tell me the meaning of your barbaric attack on Cecil," he demanded.

Seth drew his eyes away from the maze and shifted uncomfortably. Damn, he thought. "The matter concerns only your son and myself," he tersely replied.

"Not so. It concerns me, and I demand to know the reason!"

"I cannot answer the question. Let it go. My quest here in England is over. You may choose to believe what I have told you or not. It must be to your undying regret that you have sired such a weakling as Cecil. I have fulfilled my mother's request. I shall leave in the morning," Seth said, and bowed to take his leave. "You may return this to Cecil. It belongs to him. I found it in the woods." Seth handed the button to his grandfather and left the room. He stood a moment in the corridor of the upper hall. He would seek out Angus and leave as soon as possible.

The Earl of Chathram sent a request for his son's presence in his chambers immediately after Seth's departure.

Wilkins returned and informed the earl that Lord Cecil was indisposed and unable to attend him.

The earl rose from his seat with a scowl. "I shall see him, now."

Wilkins hesitated. Shifting uncomfortably, he began to address his aged master. "Your lordship, there's been an unfortunate incident. It seems some, er, stray shots were fired, killing the horse from under the American Mr. Blakewell. Apparently one shot just missed him. I've just heard of the incident. The entire hunt party is at fever pitch and the accounts change by the minute."

The old earl looked aghast. "My God! Take me to Cecil. Let us learn what he knows of the incident."

These events were taking their toll, and Wilkins actually assisted his master by taking his arm, a gesture never before offered.

Leaving Wilkins at the door, the earl entered Lord Cecil's room, and found his son settled in a chair with his jacket removed and his shirt open. Cecil's valet was carefully administering to a bruised face, swollen lip, and fast-closing eye. Cecil glanced up at his father and frowned.

The Earl of Chathram shook his head and waved off the attending servants. "What was behind the altercation? I had the unfortunate opportunity of clearly viewing it from my window. You made less than a good showing of yourself."

"How in the devil should I know? That damn American, whom you graciously invited to attach himself to us, attacked me for no apparent reason. The man is mad, belongs in Bedlam. I want him removed from Chathram as quickly as possible," Cecil spat.

"Why should he make an unprovoked attack? Did you have words? Was it over Miss Marshall?" the earl asked.

"Miss Marshall? What in the devil would she have in this? You've forbidden Anthony's suit, for which I assure you I am quite grateful. What does the uncouth American have in connection to that, unless . . ." His words trailed off.

Chathram slowly walked around his son, regretting his question concerning Miss Marshall. "I hear he was shot at and his horse killed out from under him."

"So I hear, but that has nothing to do with the fact he attacked me. The man is insane. He perhaps has more enemies, justly earned I'd wager," Cecil replied, rubbing his hand on his swollen jaw.

The earl continued his slow perusal of the room. "I am embarrassed that such a thing should happen in my home, under my protection, to one of my guests," he said while picking up the discarded coat worn by his son. Evans is getting careless, he thought as he placed the jacket on a chair, carefully noting the crested buttons and especially the missing one. Fury flushed in his face. He walked to stand once more before his son. Looking down at Cecil with disdain, he handed him the button. "Mr. Blakewell returned this to me.

It was found in the woods; perhaps that is why you were attacked," he murmured, leaving a speechless Cecil to wonder how much his father knew.

The riders had returned, and word of the shocking incident was quickly related to those who had ridden farther afield. It could be debated whether the death of such a fine stallion was to be more regretted than the near miss on the life of the rather unconventional American.

Seth was intercepted and questioned at every turn. He found Angus at the traditional breakfast in the great hall. Angus was busily engaged in conversation with the blushing Lady Markham. Hoping to get his friend aside to discuss their departure proved impossible. The guests clustered around him with a multitude of questions.

"I say, there seems to be a debate as to whether it was directed at you or a mere stray shot from a poacher," Lord Dunning said.

Annemarie, standing among the group, spoke up rather hotly. "Who would want to shoot him? Surely, it was an accident!" She could not bring herself to believe otherwise. The idea of a provoked attack had ominous overtones and raised questions of any possible motive.

"Maybe they were stray shots, because there were two. One can only put it as shots gone amiss. Surely no one could miss from such close range, but remember one killed my horse," Seth answered with icy reserve.

Desiring to make his escape from the excited chamber, he was relieved to see the earl's butler enter the large hall. The dignified servant requested Seth's appearance, once more, in Lord Blakewell's chambers.

Seth nodded his agreement and raised his eyes, catching Miss Marshall's pale face and wide eyes. She has been frightened by the episode, he thought, and he longed to comfort her. A sympathetic light shone from his eyes before he turned to go. Annemarie watched him stride from the room. She had seen his tender look and felt the sudden desire to fly into his arms.

Moments later, Seth was seated next to the elderly grandfather in chairs that flanked the fireplace. Chathram was pale and agitated. His hands trembled slightly. Seth instantly regretted his outspoken manner during his previous conversation. He had undoubtedly allowed his anger to take hold. The old gentleman now carried more heartache than should come to a man his age.

The earl looked sharply over to the capable gentleman and felt a certain pride in the young man, a feeling he had not felt since John had been with him. The Earl of Chathram had recognized Seth's claim earlier, and knew without lingering doubt Seth was, in truth, his grandson.

"You must not depart immediately. It would seem as though you were chased away. Your attendance at the ball will please me. I have guests from the vicinity attending, as well as those staying here in the manor. We would not wish it thought that you are a coward. You can easily leave tomorrow without much speculation arising."

Seth crooked an eyebrow. "I care little of what anyone thinks."

"What of Miss Marshall? I rather thought you were bound to woo the lady. I have forbidden her marriage to Anthony, as well you know. Do you give up so easily?" Lord Blakewell asked.

Seth sat in silence. A gleam entered his smoky eyes and he softly laughed. "Your argument is overwhelming. I shall abide by your request."

"Ah, you mean to accomplish the conquest in an evening?"

"Why not?" Seth laughed with a confidence he did not feel.

The excitement of the events of the hunt and the "accident" had created such confusion that it was some time before Anthony managed to speak to Anne. He found her in the dining hall, where a lavish hunt breakfast was laid out for the guests, and asked to speak privately with her.

"Anne, please come with me a moment," Anthony whispered, placing a hand on her arm. His voice indicated the same concern she had seen earlier when she looked up into his thin face and saw the pain in his eyes.

"Of course, Tony. What is wrong?" Annemarie asked, falling in step with him. She had a long stride but found herself scurrying to keep up with him. She glanced at his stern expression and was mystified by his obvious distress.

Anthony was silent and moved aside to allow her to precede him into the empty library. He softly closed the door, paused, and turned to her with a shrug. "Grandfather is livid! He has refused permission for me to marry. I am amazed, for I know he loves you dearly," he began. "Perhaps that is why," he added bitterly.

"Refused?" she whispered. "But my father will—"

"The old man is presently speaking with your father on the matter. Oh, Anne, I am sorry. But my gambling debts have enraged him. In fact, he is planning to send me to America with that heathen Blakewell. For the life of me, I don't understand. Apparently Mr. Seth Blakewell has vowed to make a man of me by subjecting me to the rigors of the wilds."

Anne stood in astonished silence, her mind racing over Anthony's words. She thought of Blakewell's pursuit. Was he behind these events in order to sweep aside all obstacles to her hand?

"Anne, I'm sorry. Since it hasn't been announced, it shouldn't cause you much embarrassment. Although I imagine your mother has probably dropped not-so-veiled hints of such a 'brilliant match' to several friends," he said, running his hand through his carefully arranged hair.

"Great heavens, Anthony, it's not done. But to reassure you, I'm not hurt or disappointed for that matter, although I was becoming quite accustomed to the idea," Anne said, placing a hand on his arm. "Do not worry for me."

" 'Tis not only that. I would not wish to cause you any pain, and that you must know. It is just that I cannot understand Grandfather. Why in the devil should that damn, rough American hold sway over him? Who does he think he is, ordering my life about as if he had a right? It is all very strange. Imagine Grandfather agreeing? It's beyond comprehension."

Anne's thoughts turned to her parents in distress. Her father would be furious and her mother unbearable. She shut her eyes. The fault of the refusal of consent by the old earl would be placed at her doorstep. Imagining the harangue, Anne shuddered. "Well, Tony, there's nothing I can do. I accept your grandfather's decision. Have you lost vast sums?"

"Ah, actually, yes. Lord Charling . . . It's of no concern for you, but I fear if I am to ever receive my inheritance, I'll have to abide by my grandfather's wishes."

"Yes, I suppose so. What does your father say?"

"Nothing. That's what's so strange. He was furious in London, when he heard of my losses. He brought me back to Chathram enraged. I thought he felt the marriage might settle me. Oh, Anne, it might have done so. Now I'm to languish in some godforsaken wilderness, felling trees or some damn thing,'' Anthony said, piercing the air with his hand and pacing the room in frustration.

Anne watched him. He seemed so pitiful. Lord have mercy, she thought. A stint of chopping wood or a swift kick in the seat of his backside was what he needed. Adversity might just be the making of you.''

"You too?" he snapped. "I thought I had an ally in you!"

"Tony, you do. Think! You're twenty-four years old. It's time you assume responsibility for your actions. I don't envy such a tutelage under Mr. Blakewell. In fact, I also find the whole thing beyond comprehension.''

"So do I. Lord, that man must have some kind of power over Grandfather.''

Anne shook her head in disbelief. She reached up and gave Anthony a kiss on his cheek. "All will come about. You'll see.''

Tony stood defeated as Anne left the room. She decided to return immediately to Sutton Hall, where some sanity reigned.

Squire Marshall was the last of the parade of visitors ushered by Wilkins into the presence of the Earl of Chathram. The earl was seated in a wing chair and indicated the opposite one for Marshall. He offered him a glass of port and Wilkins left the men after serving them.

"Marshall, I'm refusing to allow your daughter to saddle herself with the ne'er-do-well I call my grandson. He must mend his ways first,'' Lord Blakewell said, coming directly to the point.

Like his daughter, upon hearing the news, he was stunned. He was speechless, and his glass shook as a tremor ran through his body. Marshall thought of Caroline's reaction and shuddered. He held little personal respect for young Lord Blakewell and doubted Annemarie's heart would be broken.

He knew she acquiesced to marry only at the persistence of her mother, but to refuse a pledge already made was an unheard-of breach of civil conduct.

The earl watched the changing expressions of incredulousness play across the ruddy face of the country squire.

"I regret any inconvenience and hope there is no breach of friendship on your part. The decision is final, however," he said with all the authority of his position.

Marshall nodded feebly. "There'll be no recriminations," he finally said, and rose to take his leave. He made his way through the halls and out into the courtyard. He paused a moment before heading for the earl's stables, then Sutton Hall. He could imagine his wife's reaction already and braced himself. He'd not take much today, he vowed.

As Squire Marshall had predicted, Caroline dissolved into a rage upon being informed that Lord Anthony would not be allowed to marry Annemarie.

"I am shocked and humiliated. How very unchivalrous! It is not to be borne! Such a thing is unheard-of," she cried. Her portly figure heaved in indignation and her eyes bulged in disbelief. "How will I bear the humiliation?"

Annemarie sat watching the unfolding scene completely detached. In truth, her pose was, beside disinterest, one of relief.

Marshall was patient to begin with in the unlikely chance his wife would listen to reason. "Caroline, Lord Anthony has gambled beyond reason. The earl is furious and intends to send him to the colonies for a while under the care of Mr. Seth Blakewell. I cannot fault the earl; he lost John over gambling. Possibly when Anthony returns, he and Annemarie may marry," he explained.

Anne's eyes glittered a second and a smile appeared on her lips. Perhaps, she thought, I ought to marry Blakewell and go to America myself. The thought was new and took her by surprise. One minute I'm thinking, he's behind the broken engagement, and the next moment that I'll go to America with him. Great heavens, but that man has created such turmoil in my life. I'm thinking like a ninny.

The arguments and recriminations continued for some moments, finally ending with Caroline in tears, sure that Annemarie was destined to be a spinster.

"Well, now that my future has apparently been settled, I'll be able to enjoy my horses at Sutton Hall," Anne said dryly.

"You'll go to the hunt ball tonight," Caroline commanded. "I'll not allow any gossip to think we've turned tail and run."

Anne rose and stared in disbelief. "I don't give a fig what anyone says!"

"I do," interjected Squire Marshall. "We shall return to London after the ball. I insist," he said, thinking of his investment and future with Seth Blakewell. Returning to America, he thought. I must find out just when and what this all means to our venture. Damn, the man has me completely tied up. His frown was so fierce the two women were silenced at once.

16

The Earl of Chathram greeted his guests in the magnificent hall. He was dressed in a dark velvet coat and white satin knee breeches, and he sported a ruby on his simply tied neck-cloth. He looked surprisingly fit, considering all the drama of the day, and his snow-white hair sat like a crown upon his head.

Observing the elderly gentleman with admiration, Seth thought he had more mettle than ten men. No one would suspect that Lord Blakewell suffered the recent disappointment of learning the culpability of his son.

Seth sauntered into the ballroom only to be besieged by many guests wishing to hear every detail of the frightful experience. This annoyed him.

"There is little to tell. Just one of those unfortunate accidents. England is far too populated, and any hunter should exercise great care when shooting in the woods. In America we take such things seriously."

Contemptuous glances passed among the guests. They did not appreciate an American telling them of their shortcomings.

"Now, if you will excuse me . . . There is someone I should speak to," Seth said, eagerly moving to escape the prying group.

"An arrogant man, I say. Don't you agree?" Lord Smythe remarked.

"A bit of a mystery, I'm told. Could use some manners, but what can you expect from the colonists? Generally, rabble-rousers to be sure," Sir Ian Spinely said.

Seth ignored the remarks and restlessly scanned the ballroom, looking for a certain face.

The Marshalls arrived shortly thereafter, and the earl took Annemarie's hand into his. "I love ye, Annemarie, and well you know it," he said.

Annemarie smiled in returned affection and kissed his cheek. "I'm not disappointed, sir. I think you all too wise."

The earl patted her hand. "Annemarie, you're a remarkable girl."

Caroline Marshall looked on the scene with a new glimmer of hope. Perhaps, when Lord Anthony returns, the earl will grant the marriage. Taking Quentin's arm, she glanced up to her husband with a questioning look. Marshall shook his head, indicating he was equally perplexed.

Seth watched the Marshalls enter from across the wide expanse of the glittering ballroom. Miss Marshall wore an amber gauze gown. The bodice crossed in front and came to a V in the back. The gathered sleeves reached her elbows and were banded in cream satin ribbon. Her tawny hair was piled high, and tendrils were artfully arranged to show off her perfect oval face. Her stole was soft cream and draped gracefully over her arms.

Seth thought she looked exquisite, beyond any female he knew. There was an athletic grace in her movement, and the vision of her by his side only increased his determination to win her. He watched as she was claimed by Lord Anthony for a country-dance set.

Anne was equally aware of the dark-haired American. She

glanced frequently at him. He lost no time in seeking partners for the dances. His easy manner and dark good looks brought out the gushing, giggling response that set her teeth on edge. She frowned; the ladies certainly seemed to be taken by him. Once she met his eyes and immediately turned away, lifting her chin in a haughty gesture.

Smiling to himself as he noted the impact her open gaze had on him, he moved to her side.

"Good evening, Miss Marshall," he said, making a rather exaggerated bow.

Anne directed a brilliant smile at his mock gallantry and executed a grand curtsy, accompanied by batting eyelashes and a fluttering fan. "I see you are all the rage, sir. Is one to assume a moving target brings fame if not fortune? Of course, if well-directed, fortune can be an achieved object," she said, referring to the possible dowries to be had.

Seth did not understand her cryptic meaning. Did she know about his possible claim as heir to Chathram? Was she teasing over the shooting incident by making lighthearted banter, or was she implying he was taking advantage to gain what she termed fame or fortune?

His eyes narrowed a moment. She was exasperating!

"Fame, of course, and my fortune will be your consent to dance," he said with a caressing voice intended to disarm.

Looking up into his face, she thought he wove a spell, for she felt the familiar constriction in her chest. He was blatantly masculine. She looked around the room and suspected there was not a lady present who would not fall under his spell.

Just as she accepted, the orchestra ceased playing. The Earl of Chathram walked slowly to the middle of the floor and raised his hands for silence.

"I welcome you all to Chathram Manor and our annual hunt ball. Tonight, I have the particular pleasure in introducing to you my grandson, Mr. Seth Blakewell, of

Savannah, Georgia. We praise God for the blessing of his visit. It is with great sadness that I learn of John's recent death in America. The joy of having so fine an heir to my title presents me with the greatest satisfaction.''

A crescendo of voices rose as all eyes traveled to the American. Seth stood stunned. He could not believe the words. He had not sought that; in fact, he did not want it. A cold glint entered his eyes, and his mouth drew into a thin line. He should be happy, for his mother now had her wish.

He turned to Anne. ''It would seem as though your enigmatic remark had some foundation,'' he said harshly.

Anne was taken aback by the intensity of the rancor in his voice.

Lord Blakewell motioned Seth to come and stand beside him. He obeyed, but had never been more uncomfortable in his entire life.

''You honor me, sir. I am proud of the recognition, but I neither seek nor accept being heir,'' he said to Lord Blakewell, so none could hear.

''You cannot change what is fact. John was first son, you are his. I now know that to be the truth,'' the earl whispered.

Seth turned to the large assembly, forcing a smile, the effect of which was not lost on the ladies present.

Reaction varied throughout the room. Several young ladies flushed at the prospect of such a handsome gentleman now become so very eligible. Mamas' eyes lit with the same interest, and several wished fervently they had been more gracious to the man. They would see that lapse immediately mended.

Lord Anthony almost choked at his grandfather's words. He flushed to the roots of his hair. Did his father know? He was not attending the ball this evening. He had heard from his valet that Cecil was indisposed.

Confusion whirled in his mind and he desperately tried

to act unconcerned, as if he already knew. The devil, he thought, I can't simply bolt out of the room. He would have to wait until later to ask his father what this was all about. Good God, he thought, I'm to go to America with this man. Would Blakewell leave now? This was the most astounding thing he had ever heard, and he was at a total loss to gather his wits.

Squire Marshall let out an audible croak. His investment was safe! Gad, he had almost engaged Annemarie to the wrong man.

Caroline turned beet-red, remembering the rude treatment she had given him. She simply couldn't stand the rough masculinity of the man, lacking English refinement. He seemed to be taken by Annemarie, for she had seen his eyes follow her daughter. Caroline looked to Annemarie, who stood pale in apparent disbelief.

The expression, however, was not one of uncertainty. Anne believed it immediately, and her heart sank. If she were to respond to any overture he might now make, he would deem her acceptance directly related to his new position. She wanted to cry. What a coil, she would never let him think that!

Seth turned to his grandfather. "I'm not prepared to take this offer."

"We will speak of this later. I shall spend the rest of the evening enjoying the clamoring changes in the leaders of society. Doubt I could be more entertained," he said with a sly chuckle.

A wicked smile appeared on Seth's lips. "I quite agree. It will surely prove to be an unforgettable experience."

Several guests rushed to offer their felicitations.

"Knew from the start you were quality," Lord Smythe now offered.

"In America a man is judged by his actions, not his birth," Seth said.

"To be sure, Mr. Blakewell, or rather Lord Blakewell," Lady Deveral gushed.

"No, it's Mr. Blakewell; Americans carry no titles," Seth said. He caught Angus' eye. His friend gave him a raised eyebrow and a maddening smile. Seth frowned and wove his way to Angus' side. Lady Markham stood beside Angus and stared wide-eyed at the fierce look on Mr. Blakewell's face.

"And just what do you mean by that expression?" Seth demanded.

"What expression?" Angus asked with feigned innocence.

"Your I-told-you-so expression," Seth said.

"Indeed, I did say they'd make a dandy fellow out of you," Angus said, then roared with laughter. "Now what is your intention?"

"I never intended . . . We'll speak of this later," Seth said.

"Yes, your lordship," Angus said with a flourishing bow.

Seth swung around. He saw Angus' look of delight, and a wide smile broke out on his own face.

"Might not be too bad," Seth said.

"We'll see. Earl or Indian Chief, most interesting," Angus said in mock seriousness.

"Go to the devil," Seth replied.

Lady Markham, who had watched the exchange, gasped and took Angus' arm for protection.

"Yes, your lordship," Angus added as a parting shot.

"What did you mean by Indian chief?" Lady Markham asked in a tiny voice.

"Why, my dear, the new Lord Blakewell is also a Creek Indian chief," he said. Now, let the tabbies do with that whatever they will, he thought. This trip was proving to be more fascinating by the moment. He smiled down into the large brown eyes of Leona Markham and gave her hand a squeeze. Most, most interesting, he thought.

Angus' words were said loud enough to be overheard.

"Indian chief! Can you imagine?" whispered several guests.

The latest *on-dit* was passed with glee in seconds. The new heir to the Earl of Chathram was part Indian, and a chief.

"Damn savage," someone muttered.

"How fascinating, just like the man himself," murmured a titled lady. There was enough gossip to keep the *haut ton* busy for weeks.

Squire Marshall hailed Seth and offered his congratulations. "I knew from the beginning you were a gentleman of consequence. Always had a keen eye for the merit of a man," he boasted while pumping Seth's hand vigorously.

"Your powers of judgment are to be envied," Seth said with a mocking tone. His experience indicated being possible heir to the earldom did not assure honor; in fact, judging by Cecil, it could bring out the worst attributes in a man.

Anne desired above all else to wave a magic wand and disappear. She knew she must offer her congratulations despite her own misgivings.

"How fortunate for you. I hope you find all your hopes fulfilled by the recognition of your right to your inheritance," she said.

Would his suit of her be enhanced? he wondered. At least, Anthony was out of the way. His heart began to pound. He wanted to win her on his own, not because of his potential position. How would he now know?

"Will you honor me with this dance?" he asked, reaching to take her hand.

"Yes, child, do run along," Mrs. Marshall encouraged with a very patronizing smile directed to Seth.

Anne moved forward and took his extended arm. He placed his hand on hers as they moved to the dance floor. They danced with harmony through the steps, their bodies awakened by the proximity of the other. The sexual awareness could not be denied.

"You look enchanting. I have not been able to take my eyes off you all evening," Seth whispered.

A thrill ran down Anne's spine, and her heartbeat quickened. "You may reach as high as you choose, now, my lord."

"As high as I want? Whatever for? I knew what I wanted from the day I first saw you astride your magnificent Taliesin. My determination has only grown as I come to know you better," he said.

A light laugh escaped her lips. "Surely you do not choose by the way a lady sits a horse," she teased.

"It's a better reason than the size of her dowry," he countered.

Raising her eyes to his, she once more marveled at their color. The meaning in them was not hidden, and she trembled slightly.

He moved in a wide whirl, directing her steps to a small alcove that led to a room set off the ballroom.

Young ladies were warned by their mamas never to be lured into one by any gentleman. One's reputation could be ruined by such an action. The rooms were used by couples making assignations. Questionable matrons and widows bent on a little excitement welcomed their existence.

He stepped inside, drawing Anne with him. Fortunately, it was unoccupied. He closed the door. They stood a moment just looking at each other. He stepped closer and slid his arms about her, drawing her to him. She offered no resistance; in fact, she came willingly. Happiness filled his being. She felt so warm and wonderful. His lips covered hers with sweet tenderness.

Anne's mind reeled and her arms went around his neck. Her heart pounded with the joy she felt in his arms. The kisses continued with a growing insistence that engulfed her. Nothing else mattered, only that they stood clinging to each other. He kissed her cheek, whispering sweet words.

"Be mine," he said with a passionate huskiness to his resonant voice.

Be his! If only she could . . . He awakened feelings in her she had never known existed. "Oh, Seth," she whispered, then drew away. "I can't stay. It is not proper. Let us return to the ballroom; we must not be discovered," she said, and moved out of his arms.

"If we are discovered, I'll have to do the honorable thing and marry you soon," he teased.

"I thought that was what you were asking."

"Of course it is. If you recall correctly, I have already asked you to wed me," he said with a slight tension creeping into his voice.

"So you have, but I was then promised to Lord Anthony," she reminded him.

"Ah, but that obstacle has been removed, rather deftly, I think," he said.

Her eyes widened. "You would stop at nothing to get what you want?"

"Nothing, where you are concerned."

"I'm not available. I don't fall into your plans," she said, absolutely offended at his arrogant self-confidence. That he could have her merely by arranging things to suit himself.

"There are others affected by this whole revelation. You

do not seem to concern yourself on the displacement of Lord Cecil and Lord Anthony,'' Anne accused. She moved to the door. Placing her hand on her knob, she turned to the tall, attractive man. ''How does it feel to play God?'' She quietly left the room.

Seth stood a moment in dumbfounded silence. Where had he gone wrong? She did not know the circumstances that justified his action, and he could not tell her. She was not indifferent to him, he knew. He'd have to change his tactics, but how? He did not know how to play lover's games, but he realized he had been too direct. What next? He'd find a way.

Seth reentered the ballroom and took in the whirling dancers, a pretty sight indeed. But he was in no mood to appreciate the scene, and he looked to find Angus.

Damn, what a clumsy fool he was. Maybe Angus could help. Seth finally located Angus seated close to Lady Leona Markham, totally lost in conversation. He should have noticed it before. Realizing he had been too wrapped up in his own problems, he felt a pang of hurt for his friend. Lady Ansley would put a stop to that budding romance, he was sure. No American would be an appropriate match. Well, he wasn't defeated yet. He would think of something.

17

Before setting out for London, Seth spent valued time with his grandfather in conversation.

Chathram smiled at the soberly dressed young man. "No fringed buckskins, I see," he said.

Seth smiled sheepishly. "I made a point, you must admit."

The earl nodded.

"You do believe I sought only to bring information concerning my father? It was never intended for personal gain or inheritance," Seth said.

"That I know. I acknowledged you for two reasons: John was a noble son, one to be proud of, and I loved him dearly. You are his son in every respect, and I wanted to claim that privilege. I am exceedingly proud to call you my own," Chathram said, emotion trembling his voice.

"All my actions have not been honorable. Believe me, many of these events have been of my doing. I sought to coerce my way when it seemed I was not readily able to have my father's name cleared," Seth said regretfully.

"While we could not completely clear his name to the world, I now perceive the truth," the earl answered.

"The opinions of the members of your society do not concern me. I wanted you to believe my father was innocent and merely protecting his younger brother. You surely understand his desire to put the past behind him," Seth said.

"I do, and I do not fault him. Regretting, of course, the lost years. That hangs heavy on my heart, but you have given me a little of him once more. I am ever grateful for that."

"You would love my mother, sir. She is the epitome of the dignity of a superior woman," Seth said.

"Would that I could meet her," the earl sighed. "But now, what is it you plan to do?"

"I head for London. I have unfinished business to attend. I will return for Anthony and we'll head for Southampton. The *Columbia* waits to sail. Since Erskine was recalled from Washington in August, the Non-intercourse Act has been reinstated. We will have to use our mettle to make Savannah safely. I've become rather adept at evading both English and American navies." He chuckled.

"I wish you would consider taking the earldom; the family could obviously use some new, bold blood. These weak men that I call son and grandson are a disappointment to me. See that Anthony learns that a worthwhile life requires more than the search of pleasure. Let him learn that true satisfaction comes from what we accomplish. You can do it, my boy."

Seth nodded in agreement. "Cecil will refrain from any other attempt to gain the title. He is unmasked, defeated, and he knows it. Anthony has many good qualities, and I promise I'll send back a hardened man. One who can take care of himself and, presumably, his responsibilities. I must sail before the winter storms become too much of a risk."

"What of Miss Marshall? You must have the blessings of Squire Marshall with your 'lofty' position." The earl chuckled keenly, observing his grandson.

"She has refused me. Thinks I've been too manipulative, and well I have. I'm afraid I never meant to lose my heart and fear I shall leave it here in England," he said.

"I did not take you as a man to give up so easily. I was sure you'd bring it about," Chathram said.

"I'm too blunt. No fancy manners. But I mean to use these last few days to change her mind," Seth replied.

"I don't doubt you'll do it, and I give my blessings, not that my opinion means anything."

Seth's eyes twinkled. "No, in all due respect, I'm glad to have it. I'll win, if I can, and vow no one will thwart me except the lady herself."

"You ought to be able to manage that, or you're not the man I presume you to be."

Seth smiled. "I'll bid my farewell and pray we meet again," he said, rising from his chair.

"Aye, lad. God go with you." Lord Blakewell hugged his tall grandson.

Soon Seth and Angus were mounted on their excellent Thoroughbreds and heading for London. The carriage was to follow with the baggage.

"Well, friend, our journey is almost at an end. It will not be too soon before I behold the green hills of Georgia," Seth said.

Angus was strangely quiet. He merely nodded with a trace of a frown. Seth wondered what his usually buoyant friend was thinking, but he hesitated to ask. Angus would tell him, if he so desired. They spurred their horses forward on the road to London.

Squire Marshall lost no time in returning to London. The family left the next day. Annemarie had protested, to no avail. "You'll finish out little Season, girl. I'll hear no more against the plan to do so," Marshall had demanded.

Caroline was silent; she had seen the best prospect for Annemarie slip through their fingers, and she held no hope the girl would attract so likely a suitor in the time remaining. She was desolate at the prospect of Annemarie remaining on the shelf.

Squire Marshall had plans of his own. The dock venture would put him in close contact with Mr. Blakewell, and he would use every opportunity to throw the young people together. Marshall had seen Mr. Blakewell's eyes follow Annemarie, and he drew the conclusion the American admired the girl. I'll have her wed to the future Earl of Chathram, he vowed with a confidence in his abilities to bring the young people together. Marshall's confidence rested on his ignorance of Seth's plans to return to America and not claim his honors.

After settling again in Portland Place, the American gentlemen were amazed at the flood of invitations they received. Seth held little interest in these social events. They bored him beyond measure. He knew, however, it would provide the chance he needed to see and woo Anne.

While he planned to use a less direct approach, he felt slightly discouraged, for he knew her to be stubborn. After all, if she pursued her life in a manner set somewhat apart from the rigid lines dictated by society, she had to be head-strong and not as easily manipulated as her greedy father. But that was one of the very qualities he most admired in her, and the very one apt to defeat him. She'd need that determination to survive in a new land little more than a wilderness.

Angus, on the other hand, took to the social Season with an uncharacteristic relish. It seemed every time Seth turned around, Angus was off to some rout or ball. He was frequently seen riding with Lady Markham. Seth teased him about it and was roundly put down.

"Don't preach to me, Seth. Just because your suit of the remarkable Miss Marshall does not go well. Remember I hold the charm in this group," he said, turning uncertainty into a bit of teasing. He did not want Seth to realize just how engaged and hopeless his feelings were. He had an appointment with Lord Markham and would seek permission to formally call on his daughter. Fraught with uncertainties, he did not tell Seth.

Seth managed to find opportunities to be with Annemarie. He stood up with her at several balls and dined with the Suttons on several occasions.

No reference was made of Anne's refusal. Seth was cautious in his manner toward her. Treating her with kindness, he used every occasion to offset his blunder on the night he proposed. He had been too sure of himself and had offended her. She appeared distant and just beyond his reach.

Anne regretted her swift refusal of Seth. He had angered her with his superior, controlling manner. Still, not a day went by that her thoughts did not linger on him. She met him on many occasions and it was difficult to hold the necessary reserve. Her mind was full of misgivings, but her heart was full of love. She could not let him perceive that, unless he proposed again.

It was becoming difficult to hold Marshall off on the development of the docks. The man was persistent, Seth thought as he dressed for dinner at the Suttons' prior to attending the opera. Tonight, he would formally ask Marshall for Annemarie's hand. He hoped to be firmly engaged or even married before he told Marshall there would be no docks and returned his mortgage.

"The devil, what an impossible situation," he muttered. That alone was enough for Marshall to reject his suit, if ever he was successful. If Annemarie learned of his deceit . . . Damn, he had outsmarted himself, and the situation held little hope of success. With these lowering thoughts he headed for the Suttons'.

Squire Marshall greeted him with a hearty grasp and a pat on his shoulder. "May I have an opportunity to speak with you later, if that is agreeable?" he said with an intimate gleam, which annoyed Seth.

They entered the family drawing room. The ladies were seated. Seth's eyes went to Anne's, and an ache pinched his heart. She looked lovely. He smiled and crossed the room.

He greeted Lord and Lady Sutton. Sissy thought he looked magnificent, and glanced toward Anne to observe her reaction. Anne is positively glowing, she mused with pleasure. He was the man for Anne, and she sent a prayer that he would win her.

"Good evening, Mrs. Marshall. You look a picture this evening," he said, bowing over her hand.

Anne smiled slightly, for somehow these drawing-room compliments did not match the rugged countenance of the dynamic man.

Turning to Anne, he bowed and took her hand. His eyes glowed like two candles, the message undisguised and as basic. Her heart leapt in her breast, and her lips trembled. The response in her own eyes was equally revealing, and she lowered them immediately, lest he see her feelings.

A glimmer of hope sprang in his being. He bent to kiss her hand. "You look lovely, a vision I'll carry with me, always," he said. He took the chair next to Anne's and engaged her in a conversation on the bloodline of Taliesin, a safe-enough subject, he reasoned.

Seth offered his arm to Anne when dinner was announced. The discourse was light, the food delicious. Seth admired Lord Sutton and spent several minutes in conversation on the politics being waged on the high seas to counteract the war with Napoleon. Anne listened with interest. She was only slightly aware of the havoc the embargo acts were having on both English and American economies. The congenial atmosphere continued as they left for the opera.

Seth was seated across from Annemarie during the ride and watched the pale light emanating from house lanterns play on the planes of her face. The rhythm of the sound of the horse's hooves, the flickering light, and the sweet smell of cologne gave a false sense of intimate harmony. She returned his look, and no one else existed.

Seth was lost to the enchantment and started when Caroline's voice shattered the spell by announcing their arrival.

Assisting Anne to alight, he took her arm and escorted her into the glittering opera house. As soon as they had been seated, the party was aware of the interest they invoked. Several members of society nodded or waved from their boxes, curious of the company with the new heir to Chathram. Caroline took delight in what she assumed added to her consequence and fluttered her fan with a self-satisfied smirk.

Seth seemed unaware of all this. He placed himself so he might freely gaze at Anne without being too obvious. The music flowed over him, and his thoughts traveled into a world of Anne beside him at Riverview, riding with the freedom she had never known in Surrey.

Anne was entranced by the story enfolding before them, and her heart swelled with the lyrical music. Delight animated her face. Once she became aware of Seth and turned to find his gaze upon her. She smiled, but the disconcerting shiver that ran down her spine forced her to recognize that she must sort out her feelings toward him. He undoubtedly intrigued her. She dropped her lids and toyed with a ribbon, then turned her attention back to the performers.

Following the opera and upon reaching the Sutton town house, Seth accompanied them into the foyer. All agreed it was an outstanding performance and bid one another good evening.

Seth took Anne's hand and begged permission to call in the morning.

"You are always welcome, Mr. Blakewell."

"Would eleven be agreeable?" he asked.

"Yes," she murmured.

"Come, lad. I wish to speak a moment with you. I'll not keep you long," Squire Marshall insisted.

Lord and Lady Sutton bid them all good night and followed Anne and Mrs. Marshall up the stairs.

Squire Marshall ordered brandy and escorted Seth into the well-stocked library. A crackling fire burned brightly, casting flickering shadows along the walls. It was a comfortable room.

"Be seated, Mr. Blakewell," the squire said as he accepted the brandy brought by the unobtrusive butler.

They settled themselves and Squire Marshall broached the subject of the docks. "Tell me just where we are in this venture. I have not had a chance to ask before now," he said with a tinge of worry that he could not explain.

"Sir, might we put off that conversation until tomorrow or the next day? I shall take you to the site and we'll discuss all the details. There is something else I should like to ask," he said.

"Certainly," Marshall answered.

"Would you give your permission to my suit of Annemarie? I should like to make her my wife," he said, and found to his chagrin he was nervous.

"I'd be proud to have you as a son-in-law. Annemarie would make you an outstanding wife. You have my permission. Have you reason to think she'll consent?"

Seth frowned. "Not really, but I am hopeful. America would suit her."

"America? You're returning to America? What of your inheritance to the earldom?" he asked in utter surprise.

Seth was unable to answer, for he did not know whether he'd come back or not. It depended on Anthony. If the young man grew into a sense of responsibility, he would send him home, ready for the reins of Chathram. Seth had no interest in doing so.

"That lies in the future. The earl is still in excellent health. I must return, for my business needs attending. I have been gone long enough. My business is done here. I wish to take Annemarie with me as my bride," he said.

Marshall sat a moment, his thoughts reeling. "What of the docks?"

"That can still be built if we want, but we'll talk of that later. It is too complicated for this time of night," Seth said, skirting the issue.

Marshall frowned. "Caroline will not be pleased to have Annemarie so far away. I'm not sure my daughter would wish to go to such a raw land."

"Then I will remain."

The squire brightened. "You have my blessing. Best wishes, but be assured Annemarie will marry only if she desires to. She's a headstrong girl." He laughed with fondness for her.

Satisfied, Seth rose to take his leave. Thanking Squire Marshall, he left the house with expectations. Now, all he had to do was convince Annemarie. He did not like the implications. He desired her to come freely and with joy. He correctly dismissed her previous refusal during the ball as mere pique with his clumsy address. He remembered her enthusiastic response when he kissed her and he hoped he could fan that interest into wholehearted consent.

* * *

Meanwhile, Annemarie prepared for bed, dismissing Flora as soon as possible. She slipped into bed with a sigh of relief. Mr. Blakewell created such turmoil in her mind and soul that it was almost a relief to escape his presence. She thought of him and beamed as she snuggled in the covers, berating herself for her decidedly girlish foolishness. How did one deal with a man who gave one weak knees? She laughed silently at herself. She could subdue the mighty stallion Taliesin, but Mr. Blakewell turned her into a quivering, indecisive ninny.

Remembering his kiss, she felt the same warmth flood her body. Calling tomorrow! Was he going to ask for her hand? Should she accept? She was sure her parents would be delighted. Her mother would approve, now that he would inherit the Earldom of Chathram. Little she cared for that. Her mother would be ecstatic. If he proposed again, she would happily agree. No other man had made her feel this way, and in no other arms did she long to be.

18

The early sun streamed in the windows of the comfortable study at Portland Place. An air of concern pervaded the room as the two fashionably dressed gentlemen sat in quiet conversation.

Angus studied his worried friend and tried to think of some way to help. "Do you think she'll accept?" he asked.

"I have every reason to believe so. Not surprising, Squire Marshall is amenable, since I can now claim the inheritance. Isn't it ironic? An inheritance that I don't give a damn about is the means to get what I desire most. Mrs. Marshall would sell her daughter to the highest bidder if it gave her social standing," Seth replied derisively.

"I wasn't speaking of them. I know their ilk. What of the lady concerned?"

"She's not indifferent to me. It rankles that she agreed to wed Anthony at her parents' insistence."

"But if I know you, that ain't enough. You'd want her solely if she desires the match as much as you. Go to the ends of the earth with you, as the phrase goes."

Seth nodded. "That's another problem. Will she go to America with me? I don't long to stay here."

"If she loves you enough, she will," Angus said, and his voice quivered.

Seth looked sharply in his direction. He raised a black brow in question.

Angus waved him off. "We'll speak of me later. It's your problem we're contemplating now."

Seth felt a twinge of sympathy; he was afraid Angus had his own problems concerning a certain young lady, and his friend sat helping to sort out the tangle so skillfully woven.

"I've outwitted myself, Angus. I realized when I began, reprisal could rebound and come to haunt me. It seems vengeance is a double-edged sword."

Angus nodded with another pang of empathy. "We hadn't planned on your falling in love with one of the culprits' daughters."

"Yes, just as they did not plan on John living to sire a son," Seth replied.

"What are you going to do? You've got permission to ask for her hand. If she accepts, explain to Marshall and return his mortgage on Sutton Hall. Simple enough," Angus said.

"What if she finds out? How can you begin a marriage with 'I beg your pardon, my dear, but I was out to ruin your father to avenge his crime against my father?' It boggles the mind," Seth said, shaking his head in disbelief at the situation. His optimism of the night before had seemed to vanish under the light of day.

Angus sat silent. Lord, he thought, how can he? "Speak privately to Marshall and swear him to secrecy. We know he's capable of that. He'd still want an earl in his family, I'm sure."

"I don't doubt that for a minute, but I wish to return to Georgia. English aristocracy is not for me. The challenge of the growth of our new country is far too exciting for me to miss. I love being a part of it. Angus, she'd be perfect for that life. I know she'd be happy there. I can't imagine not winning her," he said, his voice soft and filled with the pain of the real possibility he would lose her. "How can I hide all this? It's so deceptive. Yet, I don't want to tell her the caliber of man her father is."

"There's a simple answer, my friend. You either love her enough to ask her to go with you, or you lose her. She doesn't have to know all. It's not like you're hiding a crime you committed," Angus said.

"Angus, we were out to ruin Marshall, and succeed we would have!"

"So we changed our minds, due to mitigating circumstances." He laughed.

"How can you think it's amusing?" Seth asked in anguished disbelief.

"Seth, you're making this a Cheltingham tragedy! You can't change what's happened. You can only attempt to bring a happy resolution to the situation. It comes down to whether you want to take a chance to have her."

"You're right. I'll ask her, then speak to Marshall," he said with more than a little apprehension. "Angus, what of you? Are you serious about the charming Lady Markham?"

Angus nodded. "But I don't know my chances. An untitled American is hardly considered much of a catch. She's adorable, so tiny and helpless, that I am overwhelmed with the desire to care for her forever. She's not the dashing quality of your lady, yet she suits me beyond anyone I've ever known. I'm going to ask. Don't hold much hope, but, my good man, I'll ask, beg, and plead," he teased.

"Good luck," Seth said.

They smiled with the great understanding they held for each other.

Seth's concern about telling Squire Marshall there would be no docks was unnecessary. Devon Sutton had the honor of doing so. Lord Sutton inquired, during an early-morning ride and a chance meeting of Sir Edward Sloane, a director of the Bank of England, about the financing of the docks to be built by a Mr. Seth Blakewell. The officer of the Old Lady of Threadneedle Street scoffed.

"The man has the means to do so. He has put together the financing but allowed the option on the land to lapse. It would seem he has changed his mind. By the way, I was surprised to see your sister's property put up as collateral," Sloan replied.

Lord Sutton was so taken aback that he sat speechless and red-faced. He could feel the blood pounding in his temples. Mumbling some incoherent remark, Sutton excused himself. He was furious! That idiot Marshall, he fumed on his ride home. He'll not get away with this. He has no right to mortgage Caroline's land, husband or no, Sutton thought. By God, I'll kill the stupid man, he raged to himself.

Arriving home, Devon paced impatiently until breakfast was served. He wanted all the family as witness to the exposure of Quentin's irresponsible act. Devon could not imagine placing in jeopardy a family's welfare on some unknown gentleman's scheme. He knew little of the American, but now held him out to be some unprincipled charlatan. Lord Sutton knew the blackguard Blakewell—that is how he now judged the man—was coming to make an offer. He would expose Marshall and the American before the entire family.

"I understand, Quentin, you have mortgaged Sutton Hall for docks that are not to be built. Tell me, whatever had you in mind? You know you may not touch those properties. I demand an explanation," Devon said while every pair of eyes turned to him in shocked disbelief.

Quentin blanched as if he had been struck. Caroline screeched in outrage. Sissy sat quietly. Anne's heart sank to the pit of her stomach.

"Well, answer me, Quentin!" Devon demanded.

"I know it to be a good investment. And I have not heard they are not to be built. I will speak to Mr. Blakewell when he calls today," he answered feebly, and a tremor racked his body.

"The man's a charlatan. Demand the return of the mortgage or I'll have you both in court," Devon said.

Caroline wept. "Is this true? How could you, Quentin? We cannot afford another of your poor investments. You have no right to touch Sutton Hall."

Marshall rose. "I'll see that it is all straightened out when Mr. Blakewell calls," he said, placing his napkin on the table. He left the room completely confused and outraged.

Caroline rose, crying. "You'll not receive the man, Annemarie. He no longer is acceptable."

"But, Mother, we should at least hear what he has to say."

Sissy looked on the scene and felt great distress for her much-loved niece. "I think Annemarie deserves an explanation. Perhaps we are seeing things in the wrong light," she said.

"There is only one way to perceive it, my dear. You have always been too forgiving," Devon retorted in uncharacteristic censure to his wife.

Anne rose and said, "Nevertheless I shall at least listen to what he has to say."

With justified trepidation, Seth called at the elegant Sutton town house at precisely eleven o'clock. Looking every inch like a gentleman about to propose, he was wearing a coat of blue superfine, pantaloons, and high shiny Hessians that sported jaunty tassels. His black hair curled out from under his high beaver hat. He self-consciously patted the pocket that held the ring he had purchased in a moment of optimism. He also carried an enormous bouquet of red roses.

The solemn butler ushered him to a waiting Squire Marshall. Seth recognized instantly that something was amiss. Marshall stood pale and trembling, a mere ghost of his usual robust self.

"Good morning," Seth greeted him.

"You may dispense with the niceties, Blakewell, and explain yourself. It has come to my attention there are to be no docks. You have let the options of the land go. Where is my mortgage?" Marshall asked, his voice trembling with rage.

Seth had been in the process of crossing the room. He halted his steps, and a muscle tightened in his jaw. His eyes narrowed a second as he nodded. "Your mortgage is now returned to you," he said, removing the document from his inside coat pocket, then handing it to Marshall.

"You never intended to build those docks," Marshall accused as he tossed the document into the fire.

"Never, my intention was to ruin you."

"Why?"

"Surely you can answer that," Seth mocked. "I think it was a rather fitting justice for the harm done my father."

"It wasn't my fault. I only tried to help. I—I never meant to harm John, only to help Cecil."

"I should think it is one and the same." Seth's cold voice carried his own anger.

"What do you intend to do?" Marshall asked.

"I came to clear my father's name. While that's not been quite accomplished, the Earl of Chathram knows, and that is really all that is necessary. I care nothing what society thinks," Seth replied.

"You're obviously expecting to offer for my daughter," Marshall scoffed, seeing the bouquet Seth held.

Seth felt a real twinge as to how this would affect his suit.

"I am. That is precisely why I did not ruin you. I had not expected to fall in love."

"Love! You fool, she'll not have you," Marshall taunted.

"Perhaps not, but I shall ask. I promise not to tell her of the perfidy of her father, and I doubt Mrs. Marshall will deny the opportunity of acquiring an earl in the family. So, if Annemarie consents, she need know nothing of my motives or your deeds."

Seth flinched, for he was lying. He had no intention of becoming the Earl of Chathram, but Marshall need not know that.

"You're an upstart blackguard," Marshall screamed.

"You were more than anxious to join the venture. You could use some instruction on the finer points of business. For example, you tossed the document in the fire without first checking to see if, in fact, it was the mortgage. You would do well to stick to your farming," Seth derided.

Squire Marshall's face took on a stunned, flaming hue as he quickly glanced into the fireplace to see the last of the document consumed in blue-and-gold flames.

"May I see Annemarie?" Seth asked.

"She has a mind of her own. You may not fare well," Marshall said, moving to the door.

"That is precisely why I love her."

Marshall turned at the door and regarded the powerful man for a moment. The American indisputably had ability to achieve what he set out to do. He's hard as nails. He may not be so bad, after all. He has vowed secrecy in the matter of John, and Marshall knew he could hope for no more. And, after all, he was to be an earl, and other business opportunities were sure to come up. Yes, Annemarie might do well to accept the man.

Seth stood anxiously waiting the few moments before Anne appeared. He watched as she came through the door, pausing with her hand on the frame. She was breathless and her eyes glittered. Glittered with what? Seth wondered.

She was wearing a buttercup-yellow muslin gown that made her look like a ray of summer sun. His heart tumbled and his hand went unconsciously to his pocket, as if to reassure himself the ring was still there.

Crossing the room to stand before him, she raised her eyes to his. They gazed at each other without speaking for a moment.

Anne was no less affected by his presence. He had been constantly on her mind as she tried to sort out the impossible business deal and its implications. What did she actually know of him? She had been in his company for only a few weeks, yet he was never far from mind or heart. Could one marry on so little assurance?

Presenting her with the roses, he said, "The sight of you fills me with joy."

"Thank you," she said, dropping her face to smell their delightful fragrance.

"Anne, let me speak directly. I love you. Will you marry me? I cannot imagine my life without you by my side. I've known it from the first time I saw you," he said tenderly.

"Appearance is hardly the reason to marry," she answered, still wary of the situation.

"It was not your appearance, though I am charmed by it. It is your honest outlook on life. You are so suited to the life I lead in America. It is a dynamic new society and I will make you happy there."

"What about this venture of the docks and the mortgaging of Sutton Hall?" she asked.

Seth took in his breath. "I've returned the mortgage to your father. There are to be no docks built by me. I return to Georgia and fervently pray you'll be at my side."

"Why did you draw my father into the false venture?" she asked.

"I cannot tell you. But I can say the reasons are behind me," he answered.

"How can we begin a marriage without your honesty? You cannot expect the kind of marriage you apparently seek to prosper with hidden secrets."

Seth remained silent. "Is not my undying love sufficient?"

"Oh, Seth, that's not the point! If we are to wed, it must be with open honesty. I cannot help but wonder that you were out to fleece Father."

"Anne, it also takes faith and belief in each other. You must believe in me." Reaching out for her, he drew her into his arms. She came willingly and leaned into the strength and comfort of his arms. He kissed her with fiery passion that sent a warm glow throughout her body. He pulled her even closer and kissed her eyes, cheeks, and neck, whispering endearing love words. "Marry me. I promise you I'll be faithful and loving to the day I die."

Anne rested her head against his chest, content to remain in his arms. She trembled. Still, her mind swirled with doubts.

"Seth, I cannot accept unless you are prepared to be honest with me. You expect me to leave with you and go across the ocean to a new land without knowing what your motives were or what you are capable of doing."

He placed his hands on her shoulders and drew apart. "I am asking you to trust me! My love will be enough. You've not even told me you feel the same. It is for you to decide."

"You can put this in such simple terms? Accept me or not?" she whispered.

"If you wish to place that meaning to it, I would not," he said, his eyes glittering.

"Love is not enough," she answered.

He dropped his hands. "Is that your answer?"

"Yes. You can change it by trusting me," she said.

"And so you can. The answer would bring you unhappiness. That is why I refuse to explain."

"The lack of an answer brings me more," she said, tears filling her almond-shaped eyes.

He produced a small box from his pocket and placed it in her hand. "This is for you. Remember the American who will love you forever."

Moving to pick up his hat, he turned and said, "I'm going to Chathram Manor to say farewell to my grandfather and take Anthony to Southampton, where we sail in a week aboard the *Columbia*. If you change your mind . . . I have mistaken you. I never believed for a moment you were so fainthearted." He stood a moment committing her face to memory, and an expression of infinite pain glowed from his eyes.

When he reached the door, he paused. "Anne, I love you."

The next moment Anne heard the front hall door close.

She stood, unable to move. Tears blinded her. She looked down at the small box she held and opened it.

19

If the British Empire was forged by men who could retain a stiff upper lip regardless of the odds before them, and the American wilderness tamed by men who could overcome adversity, then so did the Creek nation, which struggled against mounting odds and still managed to cling to its heritage. Seth, who was the son of all three, returned to Portland Place determined to put the refusal behind him. He had gambled and lost. A bitter smile crossed his face when he entered the study to find Angus.

Angus was standing by the library table folding the *Gazette*. He glanced up to his friend as he tossed the paper onto the table; it slid off, tumbled down, and scattered on the floor.

"Well, my friend, I can see you were not successful in your suit. I am surprised; I thought she had enough mettle to come with you," Angus said.

"It seems she has some reason to feel I was out to ruin her father," Seth drawled.

"Indeed? Why would one ever come to that conclusion? Surely she must realize that if you had wanted to, you would have—and with little effort," Angus said.

"Yes, you'd think she'd be grateful I gave the bumbling squire his mortgage back," Seth said in mock seriousness.

"Let's have a toast to the ladies we have loved and lost

on the fair island, England,'' Angus said, reaching for the brandy decanter.

"You too? She refused you?'' Seth asked.

Angus shook his head and flourished a wave toward the newspaper lying in disarray on the floor. "Didn't have the chance. The announcement of her engagement to some nobleman or other was published today by her family. He's a fussy, middle-aged curmudgeon. She'll remain happily in ignorance of what a real man's love might be.'' Angus bowed in modest acknowledgment of his own prowess.

Seth took the glass proffered him and lifted his glass of amber liquid. "Let us quit this land of powder, paint, and corsets. To the future, Angus, and whatever it may offer.'' Seth tossed down the contents of the glass.

Angus followed suit. "I'll be ready to leave within the hour,'' he said, beginning to strip off the perfectly arranged neckcloth.

Seth laughed. "The first thing we'll do when we get home is go hunting. I can't wait to sleep under the stars.''

Angus watched his friend and knew well the hurt he carried, but he would see that he didn't wear the willow too long, or so he hoped.

It was actually less than an hour later that the two Americans were dressed and ready to leave. Orders had been given for their trunks to be sent by carriage to the *Columbia*. They would spend the night with the Earl of Chathram before heading for Southampton.

Dressed in their fringed buckskin as a defiant gesture to all they were leaving behind, they mounted the waiting horses.

Seth tipped his coonskin cap at the amazed servants gathered on the doorstep to bid them farewell. Their swift departure had taken the servants by surprise. They had become accustomed to and even enjoyed the two tolerant, casual Americans.

"Good-bye, and may life deal well with you," Seth said.

The servants murmured various good wishes and watched the rough-hewn gentlemen ride away. "And true gentlemen they were," the butler sighed. The gathered servants on the stoop watched the two men depart on their spirited horses, knowing they'd not see the likes of them again.

Entering the busy streets of London on their fine Thoroughbreds, they were delightfully amused by the attention they received.

Angus turned to Seth. "Let's go home!"

"And not a moment too soon," Seth replied.

With resolved determination the travelers left London.

Anne remained silent, the flowers clutched in one arm and the ring box clasped in the other hand. She looked incredibly forlorn, and tears filled her eyes with the realization she had sent away the only man she could love.

Walking slowly to the hall, she practically shoved the bouquet into the arms of a startled Jenkins. He stood gaping, holding the apparently offending mass of flowers as she continued through the hall and up the steps to her room.

Reaching the sanctuary of her room, Anne threw herself upon the bed, succumbing to the unaccustomed tears. Flora was all aflutter and was therefore summarily dismissed. Caroline and Sissy both invaded her privacy and tried unsuccessfully to comfort the distraught young lady.

Overwhelming dolor and regret engulfed her. How could she have been so blind as not to see he was a mere rogue? How could she have been so taken in? He was handsome, granted, but she had been so sure he was a man of merit, a man of worthy conviction. She sobbed.

The hovering Caroline remarked, "You are still fairly young; there is yet time to find a husband."

Sissy raised her eyes to heaven for deliverance. "Come, Caroline, let us leave Annemarie now. She needs time and privacy." Taking Caroline firmly by her arm, Sissy led the tactless woman from the room.

"Annemarie, if you want anything, please ring. I'll look in on you later," Sissy whispered.

Anne raised her tearstained face and smiled to her beloved aunt. Sissy's heart ached at the puffy red eyes that showed overwhelming pain, and she departed from the room.

"I certainly don't understand why she is carrying on so. She is usually so sensible; after all, he is just a rough upstart," Caroline said, adjusting the lace on her sleeve.

"The devil get you, you silly fool," gentle, kind Sissy said, and turned on her heel and left Caroline standing in shock.

Anne was distraught throughout the day. Flora finally put her to bed. She did not appear for luncheon or tea. Sissy brought broth to her and Anne merely waved it away.

"Sissy, see that the ring is returned to him," she said, handing the small leather box to her aunt.

"I'll have it done right away. Are you sure? He seemed such a fine man. I personally was very taken by him." Sissy smiled.

"Oh, Sissy, I can't marry a man who would cheat my father!"

"Maybe we don't know—"

"Devon agrees," Anne insisted, defending her actions, for to admit that they might have been wrong would have been beyond bearing.

"Yes, but he too could be mistaken. What did Mr. Blakewell have to say about it?"

"Nothing! He said he could not discuss it," Anne wailed.

Rising from the edge of the bed, Sissy agreed, "I'll have the ring taken to him immediately."

Exhausted from the vented emotions, Annemarie finally drifted into welcome, obliterating sleep.

Toward evening, Sissy returned to look in on Anne. She found her niece awake, with her hands behind her head, staring at the ceiling.

"I sent Jenkins to Portland Place, and he was informed that Mr. Blakewell and Mr. Grey have departed for Chathram Manor and will then go on to Southampton. It seems they leave for America within a few days," Sissy said, handing the box back to her niece.

Annemarie caressed the smooth leather box and slowly opened it to look once more at the sparkling emerald-and-diamond ring. "It is lovely. I'll send it to the earl. He'll know where to send it, perhaps. Sissy, was I wrong?"

"Annemarie, some choices are just not that simple. I cannot answer that."

Anne nodded. "I know . . ."

"Let me get you something light to eat. Do try a little something," she said, stroking her niece's forehead.

Anne rose slowly and crossed the room to the washstand. Splashing cool water on her face, she sighed. "Yes, I'll eat something, then try to sleep. Hopefully, tomorrow things will look brighter. Believe me I don't know how, but now my only wish is to return to Surrey."

"It might be best to stay and take in some of the gala events, at least it would be diverting," Sissy said.

"I'll see," she answered.

Sissy had a chicken broth and fresh bread brought to Anne. Dutifully and without interest she ate it and then retired for the night.

Every minute spent with Seth was relived, and when sleep

was about to come, she was positive there was a missing element to the events, one that she intuitively knew would solve the puzzle. She could not have believed in Seth if he had been so truly despicable . . . or could she? Love was blind. Finally and mercifully, she fell asleep.

The house was silent, as was the street below her window. Anne woke with a start. It must be past midnight, she thought, and sat up. She was alert and wide awake. The embers in the fireplace gave off a soft glow as she sat in the eerie silence. Slipping out of bed, she reached for her robe and tied it about her waist. She lit a shielded taper and decided to get something to read from the library. I'll only lie and think—at least a book would occupy my mind, she thought.

The hall was dim and shadowy, with flickering sconces giving off a pale glow of light. Softly making her way across the corridor and down the steps, she was suddenly and inexplicably filled with forerboding. A shudder ran through her body, but still she continued down the steps, her soft slippers making no sound.

The pool of light from her candle lit her way, and as she entered the hall toward the library, she saw a crack of light trail across the floor from the door left slightly ajar. She paused a moment, hearing murmuring voices. Who is up so late? she wondered.

Slowly she walked to the door, and before she reached to open it, the voices became clear.

"Cecil, you're mad. I refuse to help you. You cannot try again to . . . I helped to get rid of John and have lived all these years regretting that act. I was young and drunk at the time, and have used that as an excuse these many years. However, whatever condonation I give myself, it was a crime I'll regret the days of my life. You cannot imagine how grateful I was to hear he had lived. You will not murder his son,'' Quentin commanded.

Anne stood transfixed, horrified, her blood pounding in her temples.

''He's taking Anthony to America with my father's permission. I'm alone except for the old earl, who has little regard for me. The upstart will be the next earl if he wishes. I can't allow that. I have Anthony to think about,'' Cecil mumbled in almost incoherent tones.

''If he becomes the next earl, it will because he is in line to be. You've spent little-enough effort on Anthony. I have a feeling the American might make a man of the lad. Cecil, you'll not harm Seth Blakewell, I vow,'' Quentin said. ''You can't get away with it twice. Don't you imagine the earl already knows about John?''

Cecil shuddered, merely nodded, and stared into space.

Anne's heart beat so heavily within her chest she had to gasp for air. Her father! Cecil! Responsible for God knows what! No wonder Seth could not tell her. She trembled.

The two men did not notice the ghostlike figure enter the room. Anne was pale and her eyes enormous with disbelief.

''You'll have to kill me, Lord Blakewell, for I now know the truth,'' she said.

Two heads snapped up at her words. Quentin began to rise. Cecil sat and stared, uncomprehendingly.

''He's mad,'' Quentin muttered, wondering just how much his daughter had heard. His face drained of all color and his hands shook.

Anne looked to her father, seeing him for the first time. She pitied him. He was weak and a fraud. Tears filled her eyes. ''I warn you both. You will have to kill me if harm comes to Seth. I will call the magistrates now if need be.''

There was no answer. Marshall dropped down in his chair and buried his face in his hands and wept.

Cecil finally understood the implications and knew his quest to become the Earl of Chathram was over. He rose and looked to Annemarie. ''You need not fear that he will be harmed. It is over—all over,'' he said, and walked toward her. She stood with the candle and watched him approach. Cecil paused a moment and looked at her, then stepped aside and left the room. She heard the front door shut moments later, and still she stood.

Marshall raised his eyes to her. ''I cannot begin to tell you of the depth of my regret for that incident so many years ago. But I never would have harmed the young man.''

Anne nodded. ''We will not speak of it again. Seth refused to tell me. He did not want me to know my father had plotted against his father. That is why I sent him away. I did not understand. But I love him so,'' she said with a trembling voice. ''Your sins have been visited on your daughter. May you find forgiveness somewhere.''

Marshall watched his pale daughter leave the room. He wanted above all else to call her back, but what was there to say?

Anne returned to her room and spent the remaining wee hours pacing the floor. Weighing the situation, she could come to no decision. She was ashamed of her father's role. How could she ever accept his duplicity? It was not only her happiness that had been aborted, but her admiration of the father who had spent hours with her died with the truth.

He had taught her all the things she loved the most, her horses, riding. Could she ever return to that life with her disapproving mother and her weakling father? To think he could have actually gone into a venture with the son of the very man he had cheated of his inheritance was unbearable. It was as if he had no conscience. Anne wept once more, not for her lost love, but for the loss of her innocent childlike belief in her father.

As the sky became pink, she decided to seek Sissy. Softly she traveled the hall to Sissy's room and tapped on the door.

"Sissy, will you come to me?" she called. She trembled from her emotions as much as the chill of the air.

Sissy emerged, tying her velvet robe about her waist. "What is it, dear? Can I help?" she asked in a worried voice.

"Sissy, come with me to my room, I need your advice," Anne said, and hugged her gentle aunt.

"Indeed, let us do so," Sissy said, placing an arm about her niece and walking back to her room.

When they had placed more coals on the fire, the two ladies seated themselves on Annemarie's bed.

Anne related her story.

20

It took all Sissy's discipline not to react with horror at the tale. Realizing her niece needed quiet comfort and guidance far more than hysterics, Sissy sat with tightly folded hands and listened to the unfolding story.

"Annemarie, all this must remain between us. Caroline or Devon must not know. Now, my love, what do you propose to do?"

"What can I do?" Anne whispered.

"Are you so fainthearted? I think not," Sissy declared, leveling a direct gaze on her distraught niece.

Anne stared at her aunt in disbelief. "You think I ought to go to him?"

"Do you love him? Do you want him? Are you willing to risk the unknown to be with him?"

"Yes, yes, yes," Anne cried, throwing her arms about her aunt, and Sissy laughed.

"Then I think we must be about your packing. It sounds like you'll have time to intercept him in Southampton, since he stops at Chathram to visit the earl and collect Anthony."

"Oh, Sissy, you're wonderful! Help me pack." Anne laughed, jumping up and running toward her wardrobe.

"I'll call Flora. She'll grumble at the hour but will dearly love to help. I'll not be surprised that she'll insist on going with you," Sissy said, rising to fetch Anne's maid and several footmen to bring in trunks.

The next hours were sent in frantic packing. Flora never hesitated for a moment in her desire to accompany her mistress. They worked with dispatch. Annemarie's spirits soared.

The devastating news that indicted her father seemed suddenly insignificant in the light of possible happiness with Seth. She could think only of reaching Seth in time.

"What if I miss him?" she suddenly asked.

"You won't. Love wins out," Sissy said, and blushed, for she still loved her Devon and wished as much for her niece.

By the time her parents had risen, the trunks were packed. Caroline was horrified. "I cannot allow you to disgrace yourself chasing after the bold American—"

Quentin interrupted his wife. "She has my blessings. If she will allow me—and I pray, Annemarie, you will allow me—I will accompany you to Southampton."

Anne looked at her father and saw his pain. "You may. I should like that above all else." An expression of love and gratitude shone from his eyes.

Caroline viewed the scene and acquiesced. "Annemarie, if you are sure this is what you truly want, then I cannot forbid it. I will wish you all the luck you'll surely need," Caroline said, not resisting one last word of disapproval.

"Thank you, Mother. I want to go with your blessings," Anne replied.

Finally all was ready—the trunks strapped to the carriage and horses waiting. The coachman climbed up upon his box.

Annemarie was dressed in a lovely bronze velvet traveling dress and pelisse trimmed with beaver fur. She wore half-boots and carried a matching fur muff. Her high bonnet sported curling feathers and she looked exceedingly attractive. An excited sparkle indicated the happiness she was experiencing.

"Well, I'm off to worlds unknown." Anne laughed, raising her arms to hug her mother. "Sissy, I'll name my first daughter after you, and she'll be a handful, I'll wager!"

Like Seth, Annemarie was putting the past chapter of her life behind her. A new life was about to begin, and she would face it with excitement and courage.

Sissy had spoken to Devon and received his acceptance of the marriage. Marshall had subdued Caroline and her objections.

So, with many hugs and some tears, Annemarie bid her mother, Sissy, and Devon good-bye.

Flora had seated herself in the carriage. Squire Marshall assisted Annemarie into the carriage and then himself. They waved and cried good-bye a dozen times as the coachman cracked his whip and sent the carriage forward.

"Oh, she's a foolish girl," wailed Caroline.

"I doubt it. He seems like a man worthy of her," Sissy dryly answered as she moved up the steps into the house. Sissy smiled, knowing Annemarie would find the happiness she deserved. A courageous girl, well-suited for the new land.

The journey was difficult and required several changes of horses and a stay in a rather comfortable inn.

Squire Marshall seized the opportunity to speak to his daughter during dinner at the Queen's Arms, where they stayed.

"Anne, I beg your forgiveness. My sin was one of youth and too much liquor. I will admit I used the knowledge wickedly and now regret all this has brought. Can you ever find it in your heart to love me again?"

"Father, give me time. I'll always love you. My

disappointment is in finding you less than perfect. It is not my place to judge you. Make your peace with God. I tell you, I am so very happy I cannot bear to dwell on past sins. Merely wish me well. I do hope we'll meet again. Perhaps we will come back to England. I do not know, but I'll go wherever he desires,'' she sighed, and leaned back happily.

Squire Marshall knew that was the best he could hope for and said no more on the subject.

Seth and Angus arrived at Chathram the day they left London. They spent one day with the earl and left with Anthony early the following morning.

Seth had not committed himself to return. He explained to his grandfather that he wasn't really destined to be the Earl of Chathram. He promised if he did not return, he would send back a young man ready to take the reins of that honorable position. He simply avoided mentioning Cecil.

Chathram was pleased with the young man and disappointed he had not won Miss Marshall. They would have made a perfect pair, he thought. Seth might have stayed in England had he married Annemarie; unfortunately that was not to be.

Anthony surprised everyone by suddenly taking the trip as some adventure that might prove to be interesting. He actually and cheerfully helped to prepare for the journey.

When they were ready to depart, the Earl of Chathram accompanied them to the front entrance.

"God go with you, lad. I'm proud to call you grandson. Write me; I'll be thinking of you often," he said, embracing Seth.

He turned to Anthony. "I'm looking forward to your return. Learn much that will make you the leader this family needs," he said, embracing Anthony.

The old earl stood sadly on the steps and shook his head in resignation as he waved a fond farewell to his grandson and Angus. He remained standing until they were no longer in sight and turned sadly to enter a lonely house.

The gentlemen rode on horses and made better time than a lumbering carriage. They made excellent time, and when they reached Southampton, the *Columbia* sat proudly waiting to sail.

Anthony was happy in the spirit of new adventure. He was excited about shipping out on the *Columbia*. He was greatly taken with the fine ship when first he saw her lying at berth. Seth smiled at his enthusiasm and open expressions not permitted in London drawing rooms.

"I was against this in the beginning, but you'll see, I'm as good a man as you'll find," Anthony promised.

"I believe it. That's why I brought you. You're going to be amazed at what you'll learn." Seth laughed and slapped the lad on the back.

Anthony watched with keen interest the busy activity of all the crew. Sailors adjusted the riggings and sails. Seamen worked bringing last-minute provisions aboard ship. Food supplies and fresh vegetables, fruit and water were being stored in final preparations. Captain Worth had been notified they would be sailing, since the ship's cargo had been previously loaded.

Captain Worth informed Seth of the reinstatement of the Non-intercourse Act against Great Britain by President Madison.

"I've heard! And I thought we were through with blockades. We'll see what weather we sail in and perhaps we'll return through the Caribbean. I hope we don't encounter any early-winter storms. My luck has not been running well, so count on a rough journey," Seth said.

"Had 'em before. *Columbia* . . . she's a lady that will take rough seas with grace," Captain Worth answered.

"Wish the same could be said about a certain lady," Seth replied with a glint of steel in his eyes.

The captain was surprised but thought better of answering such an obviously bitter remark. He shrugged. "That's why I spend my time at sea." The *Columbia* doesn't give me any trouble I can't handle, he thought. He excused himself to return to work.

Seth went to stand on the deck and watch the thronging workmen as the last supplies were being loaded. The air was chilly and the tangy salt air invigorated him. He would put all England behind him. He thought of Annemarie and remembered holding her in his arms. As he leaned against the rail, the wind ruffled his black hair as he watched the dock and working seamen.

Angus came to stand next to him. "We achieved what we came for, Seth. Your mother will be satisfied."

"I leave far more behind, Angus. Anne was the one for me. I doubt I'll ever find another," he said, then stopped. Straightening up, his eyes narrowed as he saw a coach enter the quay of their dock. He watched the vehicle slowly make its way among the busy workers. Finally the coach halted. Seth's heartbeat quickened.

Annemarie, flushed with excitement, waited while her father stepped out to inquire if this was where the *Columbia* was berthed. The seaman looked at the gentleman as if he were loony and gestured to the huge vessel. The bow sported a fine carving of *Columbia* wrapped in carved stars and stripes.

Squire Marshall nodded his thanks and turned to help his daughter alight from the coach. He motioned to Flora to stay put. Flora frowned and wished to stretch her legs. The journey had been harrowing, with Annemarie demanding they go faster with every passing mile. Flora felt she had been rattled enough to last a lifetime.

Anne stepped out of the carriage, looking for all the world as if she were about to take a stroll in Hyde Park. Slightly lifting up her skirts, she picked her way across the quay to the edge of the gangplank. A rugged American seaman stopped her.

"What can I do for you, ma'am?" he asked.

"Will you tell Mr. Blakewell he has a visitor?" She smiled sweetly.

The seaman blushed. "You wait here; I'll fetch him," he replied, for it was his duty that no unauthorized persons board the ship. It bothered him to make the lady wait, but orders is orders, he thought.

Seth had seen the carriage and the young lady emerge.

"Good God, it's Anne, I know it's Anne," he shouted, and gave Angus a playful shove. He crossed the deck and stood at the top of the gangplank.

"Sir, there's a lady come to see you," the seaman informed him.

Seth paid no attention but nodded as a grin broke out on his face.

"Seth, Seth, I've come. You're here, thank God! It's me, Anne," she called, standing on tiptoe and waving her arm, causing the plumes on her bonnet to wave frantically in the air.

He placed a foot up on the edge of the threshold to the deck, and leaned forward, a look of incredible happiness on his face. "Ah, so it is. What would you be wanting, my lady?" he drawled with a wicked gleam in his eyes. His smile, however, gave him away.

"Seth, you beast! It's you I want. There, I've said it for the whole world to hear," she snapped.

Seamen of every description paused and watched the

unfolding drama with unabashed interest. Seamen working the riggings whistled and shouted. Others waved their hats in approval.

"Missy, I'll have ye, if'n he's stupid enough to let you stand there," a laughing sailor called.

Anne flashed him a most beguiling smile and curtsied. Picking up her skirts, she ran up the gangplank.

Seth stepped back to allow her to board and he reached out to her as she threw herself in his waiting arms. He pulled her to him and planted a very thorough kiss upon her lips.

The seafaring audience whistled and yelled approval.

"Oh, Seth, I thought I had lost you." She laughed and cried.

"And so thought I. You're willing to take a chance on an American blackguard?" he asked.

"I love you," she said, and reached up to place a well-executed kiss herself.

The cheers and hooting continued.

"You're bold as baggage. I'll have to marry you now," he said.

"I have your entire crew as witness to your commitment. I've no doubt they'd vouch for me."

"Miss Marshall, I doubt there would be a man who would not call me out if I don't do my duty toward you," he teased.

He looked up to see Flora climbing aboard, followed by Squire Marshall.

"Take good care of her, Blakewell. She's all I hold dear. Forgive me . . ." he said with faltering words.

"I'll make her happy. I can only thank you for giving me what I love most in the world," Seth said, shaking hands with his free hand while holding tightly to Anne with the other.

Anne kissed her father farewell. They parted with amends made.

Seth stood with his arm around Anne as they waved him good-bye.

"My love, are you sure? It's a new and raw land we go to. I have thought of nothing but you. Anne, I've loved you since the day I met you. I pledge to honor the trust you place in me," Seth said as he guided her down to the cabins. He introduced her to Captain Worth.

"Set sail, Captain, as soon as possible. You have a wedding to perform as soon as we clear England's shore," Seth ordered.

"Yes, sir." The captain saluted and winked at Anne.

"So soon?" Anne asked with feigned innocence.

"Don't play coy with me. I'll not be without you a minute longer than necessary. You've run me a merry chase, but I feel that we've both won." He laughed and hugged her tight.

They were alone, and he shut the door.

"Anne, I don't believe you're here. I love you," he said with a voice filled with emotion. He kissed her again and again.

They were married at sea with the whole crew, Angus and Flora in attendance. Anne wore a cream silk dress brought for the hoped-for event. Seth thought she was never lovelier, unless it was the day he had seen her astride the magnificent stallion Taliesin. He took her hands as they said their vows, his smoky gray-green eyes smoldering with unmasked love. Anne was radiant and returned the love with her own sparkling eyes.

Later a festive dinner was held with much laughter and happiness shared. Seth glanced over to Angus. His friend raised his glass and sent a silent toast to Seth.

"She's worthy of America, Seth . . . and you," he said, taking a sip of the champagne.

Seth smiled to his loyal friend and raised his glass to him. "To you, Angus, who have sacrificed your happiness to aid mine."

Angus shook his head. "Put that aside. We live in the joy you both radiate."

Later, when Seth held Anne in his arms as his wife, he knew the future was theirs no matter where they roamed. He drew her closer. "Thank you for placing your faith in me. You'll not regret it, I vow, for I love you more than any words I could ever find to say."

"You show it very well, my lord," she teased as she snuggled closer and received his ardent kisses with equal passion.